SURIN'S REVENGE

Surin's Revenge

JOHN HOUGHTON

KINGSWAY PUBLICATIONS
EASTBOURNE

ISBN 0 86065 558 X

Front cover design by Vic Mitchell

Printed in Great Britain for
KINGSWAY PUBLICATIONS LTD
Lottbridge Drove, Eastbourne, E. Sussex BN23 6NT by
Richard Clay Ltd, Bungay, Suffolk.
Typset by CST, Eastbourne, E. Sussex

To
Phil and Sandy,
David, Andrew and Timothy.
With love and thanks for our
years together.

The story so far . . .

Oswain, with the help of Peter, Sarah and Andrew, defeated the wicked witch Hagbane. For many years afterwards he ruled peacefully over the Great Forest in accordance with the ancient prophecies.

Then came the day when he discovered that his adopted sister, Princess Alena, was actually the daughter of Surin of Traun, the sworn enemy of the southern kingdoms. A greedy goblin's desire for her birthstone forced Alena to choose between serving her real father or remaining loyal to her adopted family.

After a hard struggle, during which she was helped by the Ice Maiden, she rejected the evil ways of Surin and joined Oswain in serving Elmesh. Then she returned to live with her adopted parents in the city of Elmar.

Meanwhile, in the northern kingdom of Kraan, a furious Surin vowed to take revenge upon them all. He was encouraged in this by his henchman, Zarbid the Sorcerer.

One year later, things began to happen . . . .

Contents

Prologue

Deep in his shadowy underground lair Zarbid the Sorcerer knelt motionless before a strange vision. He could see an old hermit, seated cross-legged and hovering in a pale blue mist above a black altar. The figure stared vacantly as though in a trance. Zarbid recognized him at once. It was his ancient teacher, Malik.

The hermit addressed him in a droning voice: 'The will of the gods must be fulfilled. The time has come for you to act.'

Zarbid bowed low before this one who so long ago had initiated him into the secret rites.

'Speak, O Master,' he breathed. 'Tell me what things must come to pass and how I shall please the gods.'

'Two kingdoms now united must be broken,' the voice replied. 'You are to conquer and destroy them.'

The hermit stretched out his hand and Zarbid saw the mighty armies of Kraan sweeping across the countryside, leaving ruin in their path. He heard the thunder of hooves and the shout of soldiers. Homes burned and bodies fell before the onrushing hordes; no one had power to resist them.

The scene switched to the great city of Elmar and Zarbid's eyes gleamed with satisfaction as he watched the high walls crumble and troops pour like ants into the streets. Then he saw himself striding into the palace throne room. Three bodies lay dead on the floor, a woman and two men. Zarbid identified immediately the forms of Princess Alena and Oswain. The other figure lay face downwards.

'Kick it over,' hissed the voice of Malik. 'Look upon the face.'

Zarbid obeyed. To his amazement, there at his feet lay the corpse of his own king, Surin of Traun. And from the king's heart protruded the Sorcerer's own dagger.

'The gods decree it,' continued Malik, as though in answer to Zarbid's question. 'You are to be the victor, not Surin. He must die by your hand!'

The vision began to fade and with it the voice. 'Serve us well, Sorcerer, and you shall have great reward . . . You shall be King . . . Lord Zarbid . . . .'

Only the flame of a flickering candle lit the yellowed features of Zarbid's gaunt face. He remained for a long time pondering what he had seen and heard. Then slowly a sort of smile curled around his thin lips. He arose.

'Lord Zarbid, eh? The gods decree it. Then I must obey their wishes. And I know exactly where I shall start!'

.　.　*　.　.

It had been raining steadily for the past two days. Andrew Brown gazed gloomily from his bedroom window at the leaden grey skies and the puddled pavements below. He felt as miserable as the weather.

'Huh, reckon Noah's flood's starting again,' he muttered. 'Much more of this and we'd better start building an ark. Horrible weather!'

He wasn't speaking to himself. Curled up on the bed next to him was a floppy-eared mongrel dog called Tatters. He opened one lazy eye at the sound of his young master's voice.

'Just my luck,' Andrew continued. 'Off school with German measles and I can't even play in the garden. It's not fair.'

Tatters whined sympathetically.

'It's all right for you. You don't have to go to school in the first place. I bet the day I have to go back it'll be blazing sunshine and you'll be flopped out on the lawn. Lucky thing!'

The dog stretched and yawned, then slowly got up and joined his master at the window. At that very moment, there was a sharp bang on the floor and he barked loudly.

'Silly dog! Now look what you've done,' groaned Andrew. 'You've gone and knocked something off the window-sill.'

He leaned over the side of the bed.

'Funny, I can't see anything. Must've rolled under the bed.'

He wriggled on to his stomach and hung over the edge to look right underneath. To his surprise, it was strangely dark and all of a sudden Andrew felt very giddy. There seemed to be nothing but a deep black hole beneath him and before he knew what was happening he could feel himself slipping into it. He cried out in panic.

'Help, Tatters. I'm falling!'

In desperation he grabbed at the dog's leg. But it was to no avail and all he succeeded in doing was to drag Tatters with him so that they both fell helplessly into the pit.

For what seemed ages they tumbled crazily downwards. Andrew thought they would never stop.

But, just as suddenly as it had started, the journey came to an end. They hit the ground with a sharp bump.

'Hello,' said a girl's voice. 'What's your name?'

Chapter One

OSWAIN'S QUEST

Oswain passed between the tall sentinel stones which marked the entrance to the enchanted glade. It was early summer and the warm night air was heavily-laden with the fragrance of many flowers. Stars hung low in the sky and Elmesh's star, El-la, shone with a special brilliance. Oswain knew he was meant to be here on this night. He made his way to the Star Pool where the Merestone shone its welcome and the water glowed expectantly.

The waters shimmered and swirled the very moment he peered into their depths, as though there was something urgent about their message. At once, he saw Trotter lying in his bed. The old badger was struggling to catch his breath. Oswain could hear in his mind the badger's wheezing voice.

'It's time for me to depart . . . I go to Elmesh . . . Farewell, old friends . . . Oswain, Oswain, a new day . . . greater things . . . seek the Ice Maiden . . . seek the Ice Maiden . . . .'

Trotter's voice faded and he lay quite still. Oswain was stunned by what he had seen. A lump came to his throat and tears stung his eyes. But before he could give vent to his feelings the vision changed. He saw a woman.

Fair and slender, she stood on a high snow-strewn crag, her eyes gazing into the far distance as though waiting for something to happen, or for someone to come. Oswain felt a new stirring in his heart. He was looking upon the Ice Maiden, and he knew at once that he must set out to find her.

The waters swirled once more and Oswain saw black clouds building up ready for a great storm. The sight filled him with a sense of heaviness. He knew what those clouds meant. What he had long anticipated was going to happen at last. He turned sharply away from the pool as the scene faded. There was little time to lose.

'But Trotter?' he asked himself. 'Is it too late? Has he died even while I have been here?'

Anxious for the safety of his friend and chief adviser, he ran from the glade and sped in the direction of the badger's cottage. However, he need not have worried, when he arrived he found Trotter still very much alive.

'Thank goodness you're all right,' he panted as he entered.

'Eh, what's that?' wheezed the badger. 'What's the matter, my friend? Have you been running or something?'

Oswain flopped into an armchair.

'I've just come from Elmere,' he explained.

'Ah,' said the badger. 'And you've been seeing things have you?'

Oswain nodded and then proceeded to tell Trotter what the pool had shown him. When he finished the badger was silent for a long time before speaking.

'I have been awaiting the call,' he said quietly. 'It

is nearly time for me to go home, Oswain.'

He made to protest but the badger held up a restraining paw.

'You must not worry, my friend,' he said. 'I have no fear of death.' He smiled. 'After all, going to be with Elmesh can hardly be called death, can it? More like a promotion really, don't you think?'

Oswain nodded. 'You're right, of course. But we shall still miss you terribly.'

'And I you,' replied Trotter with feeling. 'But things move on and we cannot stop them. That is Elmesh's way. And to tell you the truth, my friend, I am ready to go. I am old, and since Mrs T passed on life has been . . . well, not the same. You understand what I mean.'

Oswain smiled sympathetically. Their friendship was very deep and he had mourned the loss of Trotter's wife almost as much as the badger himself.

Trotter pulled himself upright with an effort. A light had sprung into his eye. He pointed a quivering finger at his friend.

'But you, Oswain, you have many years ahead. Seventeen years you have ruled the Great Forest and we have known peace. Elmar too dwells secure in the West. But times are changing and Elmesh has revealed to you a greater destiny.'

The aged badger paused for breath.

'The vision shows both happiness and foreboding,' he continued. 'Such are the ways of this life. To have the one you must conquer the other. My friend, you should go at once and find the Ice Maiden—and whatever else lies along your path.'

'But I could not leave the forest and have you die while I am gone,' Oswain protested.

The badger chuckled. 'I have received an invitation, haven't I? But that doesn't mean I shall accept it just yet. Go, Oswain. I shall still be here when you return, never fear!'

Oswain smiled. 'Then I shall set out for Elmar first thing in the morning,' he said.

Because of the excellent road which had been built between Elmar and the Great Forest, Oswain arrived at the capital city of the West within just two days' travel. He had journeyed alone and without prior announcement but word of his arrival soon spread and he was given a royal welcome as he passed through the gates during late afternoon. His father, the High King of the West, accompanied by the Queen, greeted him on the palace steps.

'My, you look well, Oswain,' he chortled. 'What a surprise! And such a delight to see you.'

Oswain embraced him. 'You too, Father,' he replied.

He bent to kiss his mother.

'I am glad to see you too, my son,' she smiled. 'But I judge this is not a social call.'

'No, it isn't,' he answered with surprise. 'But how do you know?'

'I too listen to the voice of Elmesh,' she replied, looking steadily at him with her searching grey eyes. 'We must talk as soon as you are rested.'

He nodded, but before they could say more a shout interrupted them. They turned to see Oswain's adoptive sister, Princess Alena, leaping down the steps towards them.

She was a picture of happiness as she flung herself breathlessly into his arms. 'Why doesn't anybody ever tell me what's going on?' she cried. 'I've been wasting my time reading reports on potato growing of all things while my brother, whom I hardly ever see, is riding in triumph through the city!'

Oswain laughed and swung his sister round. 'Well, not exactly triumph,' he replied. 'But, yes, here I am. And it's terrific to see you again, Alena.'

'Well, well,' chuckled the King. 'This is a happy occasion. Let's all go inside and celebrate, shall we? You must be hungry after your journey, Oswain.'

It was not, in fact, until the next morning that the royal family, together with the Lord Chancellor, assembled in the council chamber. It did not take long for Oswain to explain the purpose of his visit.

'So I see two things,' he concluded. 'I am to seek the Ice Maiden. That will be a pleasant quest,' he smiled. 'But I see the clouds of war gathering, also. And that is most unpleasant.'

All were silent when he had finished. The King spoke first.

'Hrrump,' he coughed. 'Elmesh has spoken. Of that there is no doubt. And I am delighted that you should search for the Ice Maiden, Oswain. After all,' he smiled, 'none of us gets any younger.'

Oswain was about to say something but the King held up a hand and continued. 'It's this matter of war that puzzles me,' he said. 'Why should Elmesh see fit to give us this warning when he himself protects our borders so well?'

'That surely depends upon *how* Elmesh protects us, does it not, Sire?' ventured the Lord Chancellor.

'Explain yourself,' said the King.

'I think I understand,' interjected Princess Alena. 'We've been guarded by Elmesh for so long that we take it for granted. But supposing that were to change. I mean, I don't even know how he does it because I've never even had to think about it. Maybe we've got to now.'

'What do you think, Mother?' asked Oswain who was weighing all this carefully.

All eyes focused upon the wise Queen.

'I have spent many hours in the Tower of Visions of late,' she replied. 'During that time two matters of the greatest importance have been revealed to me.' She paused. 'The reason Surin has never succeeded in breaching our northern frontier is because it is protected by Naida, and they draw their power from the Ice Maiden herself.'

This news set everybody talking at once.

'What is the other matter, Lady?' asked the Lord Chancellor.

'Elmesh has shown me that the Ice Maiden has travelled north to the mountain range which divides us from Kraan. I believe this means that we must take seriously the threat of war. There is movement among the invisible powers.'

'And it has started already,' cried Oswain. He leapt to his feet, knocking his chair over with a crash.

'What is it, Oswain?' gasped Alena.

In answer Oswain strode across the room to a mirror which hung on the far wall. 'Where did this come from?' he demanded.

'I've no idea. Never seen that one on the wall before,' said the King. 'Not that I notice much these days, anyway,' he added.

'Nor have I,' said the Queen. 'But why?'

'This is no ordinary mirror,' he exclaimed. 'I suddenly noticed that it was giving no reflection. Now I see why. Look, there is no glass; only a mist.'

He drew his sword, the blade of which had been forged by Elmesh, and brought it down on the gilt frame with a resounding crash. There was a spray of bright blue sparks and the frame shattered into a thousand pieces, but not a sliver of glass was to be seen. Oswain turned to the others who watched open-mouthed.

'That was an enchanted mirror,' he said grimly. 'Someone has been spying on us. Alas, whoever it is may already have discovered much to our harm.'

'Then you must begin your quest as soon as possible, my son,' said the King. 'And Lord Chancellor, I want you to find out how this object ever came to be in my council chamber.'

'At once, Sire,' he replied.

'And we must prepare for war,' said Princess Alena. 'Surin is already plotting something or else that mirror wouldn't be here.'

On that solemn note the council meeting ended.

'Come with me to the Tower of Visions,' said the Queen to Oswain. 'Let us see if there is anything more we may discover.'

'I'd like to come, too,' said Alena.

Oswain led the way up the staircase to the seven-walled room with its seven windows.

'Do you think we'll learn anything by being here?' the princess asked her brother as he reached the door.

'I don't know. But I . . . .'

He stopped dead and stared through the open doorway in total amazement. For there, lying on the floor and just stirring, were a boy and a girl.

Princess Alena reached his side just in time to see them staggering to their feet.

'Oswain, look!' she gasped. 'It's Peter and Sarah!'

The two children clutched dazedly at each other for support.

'W .. where am I?' queried the boy blearily.
'W. . . what's happening?'

Oswain and the princess ran to their assistance.
'Peter! Sarah! It's us!' they cried.

'Oswain? Is it really you?' asked the dazed girl.

From the doorway the Queen looked on with a knowing smile.

'It seems Elmesh has returned you to us for a while,' she said. 'Welcome back, Sir Peter and Lady Sarah!'

Then the children knew they were not dreaming. They really were back with their old friends. In a matter of moments everyone was babbling at once.

By the time the hubbub died down Peter and Sarah had more or less explained what had happened. They were on their way home from school and were passing a public call box when they heard the phone ringing. Sarah felt they should answer it, just in case somebody was in trouble. So they both crowded into the box. But before either could lift the receiver, the ringing stopped. Then everything around them began to spin—and they both lost consciousness. The next thing they heard was Princess Alena's voice.

They also explained why Andrew wasn't with them.

'I don't know what a telephone is,' Princess Alena confessed. 'But it's just so amazing to see you both again!'

'And it cheers my heart to know that Elmesh has sent you at such a time as this,' Oswain added.

He briefly told them of the events thus far.

'So we're going to help you find the Ice Maiden,' cried Sarah excitedly. 'How wonderful!'

'It will not be easy,' he replied sternly. 'Do not

forget that there is war brewing and the northern territories may well be dangerous.'

'We're not afraid,' said Peter stoutly.

'I should think not,' laughed Princess Alena. 'Anyway, you must come down and meet Father. Everyone will be so pleased to see you.' She squeezed Peter's arm enthusiastically. 'It really is so good to have you back. I'm sure terrific things are going to happen.'

And so it was that early the next morning, Oswain, Peter and Sarah set out together on the road to the North—their vital quest, to find the Ice Maiden as soon as possible.

Meanwhile, far away in the city of Traun an evil sorcerer was making his own plans.

Chapter Two

THE SORCERER'S PLOT

Sneed wobbled up the temple steps as fast as his short fat legs could carry him. It was not wise to delay when one received a summons from Zarbid. Like most people, Sneed feared the power of the Sorcerer. He was wheezing heavily by the time he reached the door to Zarbid's chamber.

'Come in, Sneed,' a voice commanded before he could so much as knock to announce his arrival. The door opened of its own accord.

'I came as fast as I could, Zarbid,' he puffed.

'I'm sure you did,' replied the Sorcerer with a dry smile. 'Sit down, please.'

Sneed obeyed, his eyes darting warily about the sparsely-furnished room as Zarbid arose and made his way across to the window.

'I will make no bones about it, Sneed,' he began without turning round. 'You are the City Treasurer and I need your help. I have had a vision, Sneed. It is a message from the gods which I dare not ignore, brought to me through my own master, the great Malik. The vision reveals mighty deeds and a glorious destiny for Surin, our king.' The Sorcerer paused and sighed. 'But, alas, I do not know if he

26

will receive the news well.'

'What was the message?' Sneed asked cautiously. 'If one such as I may be so bold as to inquire into the counsel of the gods.'

Zarbid turned as he spoke. 'We are to go to war against the South as soon as possible.'

'War against the South? But surely there is no way? Their magic is too powerful. Surin will say so at once, though he dearly longs to have his revenge on them.'

'Do you think I am unaware of that?' snapped the Sorcerer. 'Why do you think you are here? Surin must be persuaded that it is now possible.'

'B. .b. .but how can I be of assistance?' faltered Sneed. 'I cannot break the power of Elmesh.'

'Pah! Of course you can't. I will see to that in my own way. But I need your support on the council, Sneed. And we need money from the bankers and merchants if we are to fight this war.'

'What you ask is hard and not without risk,' Sneed ventured. 'Not that I doubt the gods, of course,' he added hastily.

'True. But loyalty does have its rewards,' murmured Zarbid almost to himself.

'Rewards?'

'Oh, Sneed, you don't think I would ask this of you for nothing do you?' said the Sorcerer. He knew he had the Treasurer's full attention now. 'I was thinking of, shall we say, a quarter of the lands we conquer—together with half their taxes, of course.'

Sneed's beady eyes lit up. He grinned and rubbed his podgy hands together.

'Well, I think I may be able to be of assistance,' he said. 'You can count me in on the will of the gods.'

'I knew I could rely on you, Sneed,' Zarbid sneered. 'There will be the usual offerings to the gods, naturally, but I think you will still not regret this decision.'

The interview over, Sneed bowed low and hastened from the room.

'Fat fool!' Zarbid spat when he had gone. 'But he will do for what I want. And now for the next one.'

It was nearly midnight when Murg entered the gloomy portals of the temple. The army commander felt uneasy and kept darting cautious glances over his shoulder as he crept along the lofty dark corridors. He carried a sword in his hand and wondered why Zarbid had arranged to meet him at night and alone in this accursed place. He was soon to find out.

'You'll not need your sword, Murg,' boomed the Sorcerer's voice from the darkness.

The soldier gasped as his weapon was torn from his hand by an unseen force. The blade clattered to the floor. He made a grab for it, but as he did so it slithered just beyond his reach. Zarbid laughed as he tried again with the same lack of success.

'It will do you no good here, Commander. You cannot fight my kind of power.'

'What do you want, Zarbid?' Murg shouted angrily. 'Is this some kind of game?'

'Not a game, my friend, but a war. I want you to fight a war.'

Murg drew back against a wall, his body tense with fear of the unknown. He shivered against the cold stones. 'I've no quarrel with you, Zarbid,' he yelled.

The Sorcerer gave another laugh which echoed around the empty corridors. 'You misunderstand me, Murg. I want you on my side. We are going to fight a war together.'

Murg relaxed a little, but suspicion still coloured his voice. 'Who are we supposed to be fighting, and why hasn't this come from Surin?'

'We are to conquer the combined kingdoms of the South,' replied Zarbid. 'As to the reason why Surin has not informed you, it is because he does not yet know of it.'

'I'm loyal to the king,' Murg answered stoutly. 'I won't have anything to do with plots that Surin knows nothing of.'

'He will know soon enough, and when he does I want your support on the council,' the Sorcerer snapped. 'You will tell Surin that the men are restless for battle and you will agree with everything that I say.'

'And supposing I don't?' Murg answered defiantly.

Zarbid replied with a hollow laugh. This was followed by an ear-splitting screech and Murg suddenly found himself being propelled forwards by some great invisible strength. The intense darkness was instantly broken by a blazing fire which almost blinded him with its brightness. He struggled in vain against the relentless forces which drove him towards it.

'No, stop this, Zarbid,' he cried hoarsely.

At once the fire vanished and Murg ceased moving. His legs felt weak and his face was bathed in sweat.

Zarbid spoke. 'Commander you may be, Murg, but you have no protection against me. You will do as I say or I will bring such terror upon you that you will go mad before I finally destroy you. Do you understand?'

Murg gulped and nodded. 'Yes, all right. I'll do it. Now just let me out of here.'

'You may go,' replied the Sorcerer evenly. 'But do not forget this night.'

.   .   *   .   .

It was almost noon the next day. King Surin was in a foul mood. All morning he had been brooding yet again on the humiliating loss of his daughter, Alena, to the South.* How often he yearned for his revenge. If only there was a way to destroy the forces which so terrified his troops that none dare venture into the mountains which divided the kingdoms.

But he had other problems too. Before him stood Balgus, head of the secret police, known as the Cryls. Surin smashed down his clenched fist on the heavy oak table. His beard bristled angrily as he half rose from his seat. 'You are paid to do a job and I expect it done,' he shouted at Balgus. 'Why have you not caught him yet? Answer me that!'

Balgus shifted uncomfortably. 'It has not been easy, your Highness. Karador has many friends among the people and always they warn him of our plans.'

'I didn't call you here to make excuses,' stormed the king. 'I want to know what you are intending to do about this plague of a man. Another twenty slaves escaped last night because of his doing.'

'Yes, your Majesty,' Balgus answered meekly.

---

*You can read about this in *Gublak's Greed*.

'But we are making fresh plans to . . .'

'Fresh plans. Bah! I've had enough of your waffling, Balgus. I want results, not plans.' The king rose menacingly to his full height and fixed Balgus with a steely stare. His voice was icy as he spoke. 'Get Karador before me by tomorrow noonday. If you do not, then I will hang you with my own hands. Is that quite clear?'

'It shall be as you say, your Majesty,' Balgus replied calmly, though he had no idea what more he could do to catch the elusive outlaw and his band of escaped slaves.

'Then you had better get on with it,' snapped the king. 'Now get out of my sight.'

Zarbid was waiting for Balgus as he retreated from the king's audience chamber.

'I hear you are in a certain amount of difficulty,' he murmured.

'That's putting it mildly,' Balgus replied grimly. 'It's Karador's neck or mine by this time tomorrow.'

'Really?' said Zarbid in a surprised tone, though actually he had overheard the whole conversation between Balgus and the king. He took Balgus by the arm and walked slowly along the corridor with him, apparently deep in thought. Suddenly he stopped and faced the head of the Cryls.

'Listen, Balgus,' he said. 'I may be able to help you out of your problem. After all, your talents have been useful to me in times past and your death would be of no advantage to either of us. And I do have a rather special task for you and your men in the not too distant future.'

'You get me Karador by tomorrow noon and I'll return any favour you wish,' said Balgus warmly. 'By the gods I will!'

31

'Good,' replied Zarbid. 'Leave it to me and you shall have your Karador by sunrise.'

Within the hour a well-satisfied Zarbid was already carrying out the next step in his plan.

Chapter Three

ENTER ANDREW
AND TATTERS

Andrew blinked from where he lay on the floor all tangled up with Tatters. A dark-skinned girl was peering at him through big brown eyes which danced in the flickering light of a burning torch.

'What's your name?' she repeated.

Andrew stared dumbly back at the girl. Then slowly he looked about him. All he could see were the rugged rock walls of an underground cavern. He felt utterly bewildered.

'W. .where am I?' he gasped. 'And how did I get here?'

'Well, you ain't in yer bedroom, that's for sure?' said a gruff woofy sort of voice.

'Who was that?' the boy demanded.

'Me, of course!'

This time there was no mistaking where the voice came from. Andrew could hardly believe his ears. 'Tatters! You spoke!' he cried in amazement.

'Well, I didn't cough, did I?' his dog answered. "Course I spoke. Now if you don't mind I'd be rather grateful if you'd get yer leg off me ribs, 'cos it don't 'alf 'urt.'

'Oh, sorry,' mumbled the bemused boy as he untangled himself.

The girl giggled. 'You are a funny pair,' she said. 'And what a way to arrive.'

'Arrive where?' repeated Andrew. 'And who are you, anyway? I don't get it.'

The girl gazed at him with her bright laughing eyes and said, 'You still haven't said who you are. Tell me your name, and I'll tell you mine.'

'Well, it's Andrew,' he replied. 'Now what's yours?'

'I'm Tarinda,' she answered brightly. 'Want to know how you got here?'

'Too right I do,' he retorted.

Tarinda pointed above his head. Everything was pitch dark except for one tiny, far-off spot of light.

'You came from El-la, Elmesh's star. I saw you fall,' she said simply.

The penny dropped at last. 'So that's it,' breathed Andrew. 'I've come into Oswain's world again. That explains everything. Now all I've got to do is to . . .'

He was interrupted by a loud cough from Tatters. ''Scuse me butting in, like, but have you two forgotten all about me?'

The girl giggled again. 'Oops, sorry! What awful manners I've got!' she said.

Tatters gave a sniff. ''Salright. I mean, I'm only a dog, ain't I? Still I accept yer apologies in the spirit wiv wot you gave 'em. Can't say fairer than that, can I? Anyway, me name's Tatters and I'm pleased to meet yer, Tarinda. Now, wot on earth are we doin' 'ere?'

'I don't know,' she replied. 'You'd better come and meet my parents and the others. After all, you must have been sent for something.'

'They are friendly, I suppose?' Andrew inquired

cautiously.

'Of course they are,' she laughed. 'Now come on and I'll take you to them.'

So with Tarinda leading, the three set out along a narrow winding tunnel.

Tatters nudged Andrew. "'Ere, you'd better ask fer some clothes when we get there. You've still got yer pyjamas on!'

'Oh, no,' gasped Andrew. 'What a twit! I don't half feel embarrassed.'

'One consolation prize, though,' replied the dog. 'Yer spots 'ave vanished!'

The trio wound their way through about ten minutes of stony corridors before they emerged quite suddenly into a vast well-lit cave. Dozens of people of many different races were busy about their crafts. Cooks, leather workers, coppersmiths, weavers, potters, stonemasons and many others made the cavern a hive of noisy, bustling activity.

So much so that the little party was able to pass almost unnoticed through the throng.

'Oh, look, there's my mother,' Tarinda informed the other two above the din. She pointed out a dark-skinned woman with glossy black hair, clad in a long scarlet robe. She was busy putting a bandage on a young child's arm.

'Mummy!' cried Tarinda. 'It's me, and I've got someone special with me.'

The woman looked up from her task and greeted her daughter with a pleased smile. 'Why, darling, there you are,' she exclaimed. 'I was wondering where you had got to. And who are your frie . . . .'

She stopped in mid-sentence as her eye alighted upon Andrew and Tatters. 'Who are they, Tarinda?' she asked quietly. 'And where did you

35

find them?'

'Let me introduce Andrew and Tatters. Tatters is the dog,' Tarinda replied proudly. 'They came just as my dream said they would.'

'What do you mean, child?'

'Well, I waited by the Star-shaft and down they came. From El-la,' she replied simply.

Tarinda's mother turned to Andrew. 'Is this true?' she asked him. 'Are you from Elmesh?'

'Well, yes and no, I suppose . . .' began Andrew.

Tatters butted in. 'What 'e means is yes, Madam. We've bin sent. At least, I can't see 'ow else we got 'ere.'

'But we don't know where we are, or who you are, or why we're here,' explained Andrew.

The woman looked thoughtfully at the two unlikely messengers from Elmesh. 'We've heard tales of children being sent in the past to help the cause of good,' she said. 'You must speak with my husband, Karador, as soon as he returns. He will know what your coming means.' She smiled. 'But until then you must rest and eat. Tarinda will see to it.'

Tarinda took the hint and ran off to fetch some food while her mother continued to speak with Andrew and Tatters. 'My name is Clea,' she explained. 'My husband is the leader of these people whom you see here.'

Andrew glanced around at the busy community. Then he looked up. The cavern soared to a narrow funnel and high above he could see the sky through a hole at the top. It reminded him of an upside-down ice-cream cone.

'This is a funny sort of place to live,' he observed.

'Yes, it is,' Clea agreed. 'But it's the only place where we're safe from the Cryls. They're the secret police,' she explained.

'Are you gangsters then?' he responded in alarm.

'No, far from it,' she answered with a smile. 'Everyone here is an escaped slave. That's why we're hunted down and have to live in hiding like this.'

'How did you become slaves?' Andrew asked.

'It's a long story,' she replied. 'As you can see from the colour of our skins, we've come from many different lands and tribes. Most of us were captured in war when a powerful king called Surin conquered our nations.'

'Surin!' he gasped. 'Do you mean Surin of Traun?'

Clea nodded.

'Then are we in his country?'

'Yes, this is Kraan,' she replied. 'And we're inside a small extinct volcano just beyond the city of Traun. You get in here through secret tunnels and so far the Cryls have never discovered our whereabouts.'

'I wish my brother and sister were with me,' Andrew said weakly.

'Never mind, boss. You've got me,' Tatters piped in. 'Nuffink we can't sort out together.'

'You don't know Surin,' replied Andrew with feeling. 'I've been here before and seen how evil he is.'

'Andrew is right,' agreed Clea. 'Surin is a dangerous foe. But he's not without his weaknesses. With Elmesh's help we're finding ways to overcome him and Karador is rescuing more and more slaves every week.'

At that moment Tarinda returned laden with food. Andrew's and Tatters' eyes lit up.

'Phew, I hope this is enough,' she puffed.

'It'll do for starters, anyway,' grinned Andrew, eyeing the tasty pile which she laid before them. 'Come on, Tatters, let's tuck in.'

The dog gave a polite cough. 'Um, I 'ope yer don't mind me mentioning it again, boss,' he whispered out of the side of his jowl. 'But you really ought ter do somefink about them pyjamas.'

'You're right, Tatters. I do feel a bit silly,' he replied. 'What shall I do?'

'Leave it to me,' Tatters answered. He addressed Clea. 'Excuse me askin', Madam, but me boss 'ere is still in 'is 'eavenly travellin' robes. Bit conspicuous like, really. 'Ave yer got somefink more ordinary 'e could wear while we're 'ere?'

'Why, yes, of course,' Clea answered at once. 'Tarinda, take Andrew to Laris to see what can be done.'

Andrew was about to protest that it would be all right until after they had eaten but Tarinda was already dragging him off by the hand.

'Hm, suppose I'll 'ave to eat most of this meself then,' said Tatters with a mischievous doggy grin.

It was as Andrew, now clothed in a tunic and breeches, was making his way back with Tarinda that the commotion broke out. A man was running through the crowds shouting at the top of his voice. He was searching for Clea.

'Something's up,' said Tarinda. 'Come on. Quickly!'

When they reached Tarinda's mother they found her clutching her stomach in anguish. She sat down weakly. The messenger stood before her looking dreadfully distressed.

'What is it, Mummy?' cried Tarinda. 'What's the matter?'

The girl's mother looked up, her eyes wide with fright. 'Zarbid has captured your father,' she whispered.

'Oh, no!' Tarinda gasped. 'What will happen? Will they ... will they kill Daddy?'

Clea nodded silently as she embraced her daughter. Then they both began to weep.

Chapter Four

WHAT TATTERS FOUND OUT

Zarbid was feeling very pleased with himself. So much so that he almost allowed a smile to tinge his sallow features. Karador had been captured with surprising ease and a grateful Balgus would now do anything the Sorcerer wanted. He would use him later.

What made Zarbid even more smug was the fact that he had discovered the key to the South's defences. The enchanted mirror had been his idea and it had been easy for his spies to persuade a serving maid that the King of Elmar had ordered it to be hung in the council chamber. By the time Oswain had spotted it the Sorcerer had found out all about the Ice Maiden.

He brooded over the matter as he paced his room.

'Hm, so she's moved north to strengthen her defences, has she?' he muttered to himself. 'Then she knows something's in the wind. And Oswain is journeying northwards, too . . . .'

He grimaced and looked out of the window. His eyes glinted coldly as he hatched his plans. 'Then I shall kill two birds with one stone!' he rasped.

*   *   *   *   *

Everyone was stunned by the news of Karador's capture. All work ceased and a deathly hush settled over the cavern. Andrew and Tatters stood by helplessly as the people left their workplaces and quietly gathered together around Clea and Tarinda. The unfortunate messenger was made to repeat his words.

'Good friends,' he began falteringly. 'I'm sorry to bring this news. But yes, it is true. Surin now has our noble leader in captivity. He is to be publicly executed in five days' time as a sacrifice to Kraan's accursed gods.'

A chorus of wails and conflicting voices greeted his report.

'Can't we rescue him?'

'Let's storm the palace.'

'What will we do without Karador?'

'We'd better all flee for our lives.'

Then Clea stood to her feet and motioned the crowd to be quiet. She was trembling as she spoke. 'No one feels more than myself the impact of this news,' she said. 'After all, Karador is my husband.'

A murmur of sympathy spread through the assembly.

'However, we are not to lose heart,' she continued. 'Elmesh has helped us in the past when we have been in tight corners and he will do so again. How many of you felt without hope when you were slaves, and yet now you are free? Let us not panic or despair, friends.' She smiled grimly. 'And at least they won't kill Karador until the Feast of Oris. That gives us time. So, back to your work, good people, while we decide what is best to do.'

41

The crowd dispersed except for two men whom Clea motioned to stay behind. One was a lightly framed, fair-haired youth who looked as though he could run like the wind; the other was a giant of a man, with fiery hair and built like an ox. They immediately engaged in deep conversation with Clea and Tarinda, leaving Andrew with that sudden and awkward feeling that he and Tatters were unwanted and forgotten intruders. He wished they were back home.

But just then Tarinda called his name. He glanced up. All four faces were upon him and Clea was beckoning.

'Come on, Tatters,' he said with a grin. 'I think they want us after all.'

'Baht time too,' rumbled the dog.

Clea smiled as they joined the little council. She immediately introduced the fair-haired youth as Danir, and the giant as Haemor the blacksmith. Both were close friends of Karador.

'Andrew, Tatters, you must forgive us,' she apologized. 'This news has come as a terrible shock to us. Though it is not entirely unexpected. My husband takes enormous risks in order to set slaves free.'

'That's all right,' replied Andrew. 'We just turned up at the wrong moment, that's all.'

'But I don't think you did,' Clea answered earnestly. 'If you've come at Elmesh's bidding then you are here at the right time. He never makes mistakes like that.'

'So do you think we've been sent to rescue Karador?' Andrew asked doubtfully. He eyed Danir and Haemor. They looked far more capable than a boy and his dog.

'Well, we can but try,' Tatters volunteered. 'Can't fink why else we're 'ere, can you?'

'The first thing anyway is to find out where they're holding Karador,' said Haemor, 'because it's not going to be in the ordinary gaol.'

'That'll be risky,' warned Danir. 'Anyone who asks questions will be a target for the Cryls.'

'Then I'm just wot the doctor ordered,' gruffed Tatters. 'I mean, 'ow many folks is goin' to suspect a dog? Leave it to me an' I'll do some sniffin' around. See wot I come up wiv.'

The others thought this an excellent idea. There were very few talking dogs left in Kraan and none in Traun at all. Nobody would take any notice of Tatters. It was agreed that he should set off at once.

'Mind how you go,' Andrew called anxiously as his dog followed Danir to an upward-sloping tunnel which would bring him out at ground level.

'Leave it to me, boss,' he woofed back. 'Got built-in self-protection, I 'ave.' He glanced up at Danir. 'Just run like stink if there's any bovver,' he explained.

The others laughed.

Tatters emerged into the daylight to find himself on the lower slopes of the volcano just outside the city. He sniffed the late morning air and then scampered up the hillside in order to spy out the land.

The surrounding countryside was bleak and harsh. Craggy mountains, many rising to snow-covered heights, were on every side. He could make out the distant glint of rivers and streams which tumbled down the mountainsides to fill the valleys with vast lakes. They looked cold and deep, over-shadowed by high, sombre cliffs or edged with dark

43

swathes of forest. Kraan was not a soft land. He turned his attention to the city nestling in the valley below.

Traun looked as though it had been carved straight out of the rock. Not only the soaring walls but every house was made of granite and roofed in grey slate. The city was large and contained many splendid buildings, but two stood out above the rest as though competing for the rule of the skyline. One was the palace; the other, the temple.

'Me nose tells me I oughta start wiv that there temple,' Tatters said to himself. 'Right, get me bearings and I'm on me way.'

So saying, he scurried down the hillside until he joined the main road into the city.

The gates to Traun were heavily guarded and everyone was searched as they passed through. But as he expected, Tatters had no bother padding past the guards. Nobody was interested in a scruffy mongrel.

It took him the best part of an hour to find the temple. Tatters was used to following his nose but the trouble was, his nose kept chasing after so many strange and interesting smells! But when eventually he did get there, he wished he hadn't. The place stank of evil. His fur bristled and his tail drooped. 'Still, what's to be done is to be done,' he thought to himself, as he climbed the steps and slunk through the massive stone portals.

Once inside, he padded along a wide stone-walled corridor off which were many lofty archways. He kept to the main route until it opened out suddenly into a large triangular arena enclosed by three soaring walls. In each corner was a grotesque stone statue of simply enormous height. Tatters

44

had to crane his neck to see the tops. Although the sky was visible, the whole arena was bathed in giant shadows thrown by these statues.

'So these are the gods of Kraan,' thought Tatters.

He glanced around. In the centre of the arena stood a high raised dais on top of which rested a stone slab. The dog trotted across to it but the place felt so evil that he did not even venture up the steps. He turned and retreated the way he had come.

'Nah then, mate. Use yer noddle,' he said to himself. 'You ain't gonna find nuffink in 'ere 'cos there ain't no people 'ere. So you'd better sniff some out, 'adn't yer?'

He retraced his steps along the corridor until he suddenly picked up a particularly nasty human scent.

'Reckon that's the baddie, chum,' he muttered and began to follow it down one of the side corridors. He had gone only a short way when his keen ears picked up voices. Slowly he crept forwards, his nose to the ground. Soon he could hear the conversation quite clearly.

'. . . but assassinate Surin?' protested one. 'That's surely asking too much, Zarbid?'

'More than your own life?' spat back the other. 'A bargain is a bargain, Balgus. I have captured Karador. I want you to kill Surin.'

'But he's the king,' Balgus protested weakly.

'Only for the moment,' Zarbid replied swiftly. 'The gods have decreed a change. I am to rule. Nothing can prevent it. The only question is as to who will be counted as my friends when I come to power.'

There was no reply.

'I could, of course, release Karador right now,'

continued Zarbid. 'And you would be food for the carrion by this time tomorrow.'

Balgus found his voice again. 'No, don't do that,' he said hastily. 'I. . .I'll agree to what you say.'

'Good. Then you will sign this document to that effect. I don't want you going back on your word once Karador is dead. Any betrayal and I'll present this to Surin and you'll be put to death as a traitor.'

Tatters heard the scratching of a pen. He nosed a little closer.

'Now then,' continued Zarbid. 'I will instruct you as to when and where I want the assassination carried out. It may be here or it may be when Surin has overrun the South. In the meantime you will say nothing to anybody. Is that clear?'

'Perfectly,' Balgus replied thickly.

'Then you may go.' He paused. 'Oh, and Balgus, you may be sure that I will keep Karador quite safe until the Feast. I shouldn't try looking for him if I were you.'

Tatters heard the clump of Balgus' footsteps retreating from Zarbid's room.

'Well now,' he growled to himself, 'there's a turn up for the book. Old Zarbid there's after the throne. And he's got Karador. I'd better get a shifty at this old cove.'

Very cautiously he stuck his nose around the door. He was looking into a study of sorts and there, seated at the desk, was a bitter-faced man clad in a dark hooded cloak. His eyes were hard and his lips tight. Tatters didn't like him one bit.

'Time I was off, I think. But that's the bloke to watch. I'd better tell the others.'

With that he left the hateful temple and began to retrace his tracks through the streets. It had been a good morning's work.

Feeling rather pleased with himself Tatters followed his route back without much concern. Which is why he rounded a corner without looking where he was going—and suddenly found himself in big trouble.

His path was blocked by a pack of about a dozen of the largest, meanest looking cats he had ever seen. These were not house pets but fierce wild-cats with vicious jaws and cruel claws. He knew at once that he would be no match for them.

The leader of the pack hissed sharply and before Tatters could so much as turn they encircled him and began to close in for the kill.

'That's torn it,' he muttered. 'A right pickle I've got meself into this time. Now what do I do?'

Chapter Five

THE COUNCIL DECIDES

Tatters' hackles rose. He crouched low and growled menacingly. Every sinew in his body tensed for action.

'Go for the big 'un,' he thought. 'It's yer only chance.'

He bared his teeth and made a threatening snap at the leader. The huge cat spat back and slashed the air with razor sharp claws. Tatters recoiled with blood on his nose.

It was the signal to the other cats. With ferocious howls they leapt upon the dog from all sides. He was overwhelmed by their sheer weight and fell twisting and writhing to the ground. They were too much for him and he sensed he had only moments left to live.

But just as he was expecting the worst, the air was suddenly filled with the barking and baying of dogs. His attackers hesitated and looked up. To Tatters' amazement a large pack of hounds was charging down the street towards them at full pelt.

'Tally-ho, chaps,' cried the leader. 'After them.'

'Well, blow me down,' gasped Tatters as he struggled to his feet. 'It's only the household cavalry come to the rescue!'

The cowardly wild-cats needed no convincing. One glimpse of the hounds was enough and with angry screeches they promptly fled in all directions.

The lead hound bounded to a halt as he reached Tatters. 'I say, old chap,' he panted in doggy language. 'Are you all right? Not too badly injured, I hope?'

Tatters gave himself a quick once-over. He was bleeding in a few places but nothing serious. 'No, t'ain't too bad,' he said. 'All fanks to you. I thought I was a goner just then. Right grateful to yer, I am.'

'Think nothing of it, old boy,' the hound replied. 'All in the line of duty and all that, don't you know? But, I forget my manners, we haven't been introduced properly.'

'Well, my name's Tatters. Wot's yours?'

'Oh, well, actually it's Hercules,' he answered.

'Then, 'Ercules, I'm right pleased ter meet yer,' said Tatters with a grin.

'Visitor to these parts, I presume?'

'Er, yeh, s'right. Just visitin',' Tatters replied guardedly.

The hound was curious.

'None of my business, I suppose, but it's risky travelling these streets alone. I'll call my chaps off and we'll escort you to your destination,' Hercules offered.

Tatters looked the hound over and decided he could trust him. 'Well, now, that's mighty civil of you,' he said. 'I don't fancy another dust-up with that lot.'

So Tatters found himself in the company of the hounds and sharing his quest with them. He soon learned that they were no friends of Surin or

Zarbid. In fact, Hercules explained, it was Zarbid who was largely responsible for the dogs losing their ability to communicate with humans. He was tremendously excited to learn that Tatters could still do so.

'I say, old bean, what a stroke of luck we found you. You know, you could be a real asset to our pack. Tell you what, I know you're not of our breed and all that, but I could put your name up for election as an honorary member. What d'you think?'

Tatters laughed. 'Very kind of you, 'Erc, but I don't fink I'd fit in some'ow. But fanks fer the offer, all the same.'

'Pity. But never mind,' his new-found friend replied. 'Still, we'll try to help you with your quest if we can. Keep our noses to the ground and all that.'

'And if I can put in a good word fer yer wiv 'umans, I will,' promised Tatters.

By now they were in sight of the city gates.

'Better not go any further with you, old boy,' said Hercules. 'Bit too conspicuous.'

Tatters agreed and after saying a grateful goodbye to the pack, he slipped unnoticed out of the city and into the open countryside.

Everyone was eager to hear his news when he reached the safety of the underground cavern. Pleased at being the centre of attention, he recounted his adventures in as much detail as possible.

'Well done, Tatters,' enthused Andrew when he had finished.

'This is very interesting information,' Clea murmured. 'So Zarbid is after the throne, eh? And he's the one holding my husband somewhere.'

'It must be in the catacombs,' said Haemor.

Clea nodded. 'I agree. But it won't be easy finding him in that maze. People lose their way for days in those tunnels. There are just so many of them.'

'We need to get hold of that document, as well,' Danir reminded them.

'And find a way of warning the South of war,' added Tarinda.

'There's so much to think about,' Clea sighed. 'We need some wisdom. I think we will enquire of Elmesh.'

.   .   *   .   .

Surin's desire for revenge on the South ran very deep. He was an arrogant, ruthless warrior-king, and the defeat of his plans had injured his pride. Long had he sought for a way to avenge himself. But Surin knew too well the formidable protection which Elmesh had thrown across the mountain range. If it would not have stopped him from attempting an attack, it certainly did his men. All of them had a dread of what dwelt in those lofty peaks and passes.

This Zarbid knew, for Surin had often confided in the Sorcerer. And Zarbid, who for other reasons wished the destruction of the South, had carefully stoked the smouldering hate within the king. He judged now that the time was ripe. Indeed the gods Igur, Damil and Oris said so.

Late that afternoon the council met in the palace. Surin was pleased with the capture of Karador. At least that was one problem dealt with and the outlaw would not set any more slaves free. He liked Zarbid's idea of executing him at the Feast of Oris.

It would go down well with the crowds, as well as warning others not to try anything similar.

In a good frame of mind he motioned the members of the council to be seated as he strode into the chamber.

'I have called this meeting at Zarbid's request,' he explained. 'He has a message from our gods.'

Without further ado the Sorcerer stepped into a space on the floor. Saying nothing, with deft strokes he drew a triangle on the floor with a long black wand. In one corner he placed a gold coin, in another an ear of corn and in the third a curved dagger. Then he uttered a long moaning spell.

There was a sudden flash. The onlookers blinked in surprise. Gone were the coins, the corn and the dagger. All that remained in the centre of the triangle was a dark pool of blood.

'The gods speak!' Zarbid cried triumphantly. 'They have heard our prayers and the longings of their faithful servant, King Surin. And now they stir themselves to answer. Revenge shall be yours, O King! Prepare for war. The South shall fall before your sword, O Mighty One!'

With that the Sorcerer returned to his seat.

Surin's eyes glowed. He spoke intensely. 'You all know my humiliation,' he said. 'The frustration that burns within me. What think you of this omen? Is it true?'

Sneed, Murg and Balgus each glanced nervously at Zarbid. The Sorcerer's face gave nothing away.

'Balgus, speak,' ordered the king.

'I believe we should heed the omen and make ready for war,' he replied.

'I, too,' ventured Sneed quickly.

The king nodded with grim interest. 'Really?

And the bankers will pay up, will they?' he demanded.

'Y . . . yes, your Majesty. I'm sure they will if I say so,' the City Treasurer answered.

Surin shifted his steely gaze on to the commander of the army. 'What say you, Murg? Will the men fight?'

'Yes, your Majesty,' he replied with an anxious glance at Zarbid. 'Indeed, Sire,' he went on quickly. 'They are restless for war. It would be good. In fact, it would be the best poss . . . .'

'Enough, Murg,' ordered the king. 'Strange indeed that you should all agree so readily.' His eye fell upon Zarbid, but the Sorcerer was apparently lost in deep thought.

'What has become of your fear of the mountains all of a sudden?' he demanded. 'It is most unusual.'

'I believe I can answer that, Sire,' said Zarbid. 'It is the gods. They have taken away the fear from our hearts. It is a miracle, and a foretaste of our victory.'

'But what of the enemy's forces?' Surin questioned. 'Fear may go but fact remains. Some unknown power prevents us from crossing the mountains. What is to be done about that?'

Zarbid gave a thin-lipped smile. 'The gods have revealed to me the enemy's secret,' he disclosed. 'There is a woman. She is known only as the Ice Maiden but she wields great power. Even now she stalks the mountain ranges. Deal with her and the way is open.'

'And how do you propose we do that?' sneered Surin.

'I have a way,' replied the Sorcerer mysteriously. 'More than that, Sire, I shall not only capture this Ice Maiden but I shall use her to lure Oswain to his doom. For I know that even now he searches for her.'

Surin's eyes gleamed. The desire for revenge welled up within him like a fountain of dirty water.

'Does he, indeed,' he whispered. 'Then it shall be as the gods say, Zarbid. Bring me this Ice Maiden and we go to war at once.' He addressed the others. 'Raise the troops. We prepare for war and for victory!'

'For war and for victory!' the others echoed. Perhaps the mission was not such a foolish idea after all.

Before night had completely fallen, Zarbid and six of his priests had set out towards the mountains. On their shoulders the priests carried an empty coffin.

Chapter Six

INTO THE MOUNTAINS

Oswain, Peter and Sarah decided from the outset that they would travel in disguise because of the danger of their mission. So they dressed as common travellers, carrying with them what food and shelter they needed together with a few tools which would make them look like wandering tinkers.

However, Oswain did carry his sword under his cloak and, Sarah noticed, he wore a ring into which was set a crystal which had once belonged to the Ice Maiden. She smiled to herself but said nothing.

They travelled by horseback and followed the northward road which ran beside the banks of the River Til. Normally this would have been a pleasant journey with many stops to admire the scenery, but their mission was urgent and they halted only once, in order to eat lunch. Each knew that if they failed to find the Ice Maiden, or if any evil befell her, then war was imminent.

Oswain said little on the journey. He knew better than Peter and Sarah just how powerful Surin was. If the defences were broken the South would be hard-pressed to hold out against an attack. And Surin would attack. His burning desire for revenge would see to that.

The horses carried them steadily northwards towards the huge mass of the mountain range which divided the kingdoms. Somewhere in those high reaches dwelt the Ice Maiden.

Dusk was falling by the time they reached the northernmost village in the kingdom, a tiny hamlet called Tillevan, nestling under the bulk of the mountain. Here they stopped for the night, grateful for the welcoming hospitality of the local innkeeper, Rolan, and his wife Suen.

Oswain judged the innkeeper to be a good man and, after supper, gave him charge of the horses until they should return from the mountains.

'The road ends here,' he explained to his companions. 'From now on we shall have to go by foot.'

Sarah groaned, but then added brightly, 'Ah well, at least we won't get saddle-sore.'

'No, we'll just have foot-ache, leg-ache, back-ache and shoulder-ache,' retorted her brother. 'Don't forget we've got to carry everything ourselves from now on. And have you seen how high these mountains are?'

His sister grimaced.

Oswain laughed. 'Yes, but that's tomorrow. Let's enjoy a good night's rest first shall we?'

'I'm ready for it,' said Sarah yawning.

They all agreed and soon turned in for the night.

But, in spite of her tiredness, Sarah just couldn't sleep. She lay for a long time on her bed gazing out of the window at the night sky.

'How lovely the stars are,' she thought. 'And El-la is the loveliest of them all.'

Elmesh's star hung low, a radiant jewel of resplendent silver eclipsing all the stars surrounding it.

Its light comforted Sarah. She began to think about the Ice Maiden and to imagine what was going to happen when they found her.

The star-spangled sky sparkled more brightly than ever. Sarah's eyes grew misty. She felt the stars drawing closer. Into her room they seemed to dance and shimmer. Then a jingling sound like a crystal chandelier rattling in the wind filled her ears. It rose to a crescendo until it sounded like an eerie cry of anguish. The lights spun dizzily. Then one by one they began to go out. Soon there was nothing but blackness.

A deep buzzing sound filled the room, threatening, like thousands of angry wasps let loose. Sarah watched as slowly an ominous red star arose on the far horizon. Its crimson glow spread like blood across the earth beneath and the air was filled with the screeching of metal.

'No, it mustn't be!' gasped Sarah. 'We must stop it happening.'

Just then she heard a dog barking.

The noise woke her from her dream. For a moment she wasn't quite sure where she was. Then she heard the squeal of a cat and the clatter of bins followed by the bark of the innkeeper's dog. She peered through the window. The stars were still there.

'Thank goodness for that!' she sighed with relief, and promptly fell into a deep slumber for the rest of the night.

The morning was crisp and fresh, sunny, with a light breeze from the south. After a cheerful and satisfying breakfast they made their departure. Oswain left strict instructions with the innkeeper that if they were not back within three days he must send word to Elmar as quickly as possible.

The first part of their journey was up a steep track which rose immediately behind the village. It took them the best part of an hour to reach the top of what Peter described as 'a dirty great lump of rock'. There they rested for a while. Already Tillevan looked like a toy village nestling far below, and the silver thread of the River Til wound into a hazy distance of pastel-shaded woods and meadows.

'Doesn't it look beautiful?' Sarah enthused once they had recovered their breath.

'It's quite a view,' her brother nodded. 'What d'you think, Oswain?'

'I agree,' he replied. 'But, alas, it won't be for much longer unless we find the Ice Maiden. Come on, we must keep moving.'

With that they turned to face the vast mass of the mountain range and began their ascent.

All morning they climbed, so that by lunch-time they were deep into the range. Valleys stretched into the distance on all sides, streams cascaded over precipices in roaring waterfalls which gleamed like molten silver in the sunlight, steep green slopes intermingled with long grey scree runs fell away from beneath high craggy buttresses into pockets of mist far below. And above them stretched the awesome snow-covered peaks where somewhere dwelt the Ice Maiden.

Lunch finished, the trio made their way up a steadily-rising pass and it wasn't long before they found themselves scrunching through snow. Each of them felt their excitement growing with every step they took upwards.

'I wonder where we'll find her?' puffed Peter. 'Do

you think she even knows we're coming? I mean, she could be anywhere.'

'I'm sure Elmesh has made known to her our coming,' replied Oswain. 'She'll be waiting for us, don't worry.'

'She appeared from a pillar of ice last time,' Sarah reminded them. 'Do you think we should keep a look out for one?'

'Can do,' Peter answered. 'But she might do it differently this time. No knowing with Ice Maidens!' he joked.

But though they tramped all afternoon they saw nothing to indicate the whereabouts of the Ice Maiden. Tiredness set in and the children's spirits began to droop.

'I don't think we're ever going to find her like this,' wailed Sarah. She waved her hand at the vast whiteness all around them. 'It could take us years to search all this lot.'

Peter was about to agree with his sister but a glance at Oswain made him hold his tongue. The ruler of the Great Forest was looking very determined indeed. They plodded on in silence.

But for all Oswain's determination nothing changed except that they ascended higher and the light began to fade. Soon the setting sun was tinging the peaks with pink and the shadows were falling fast. With a sigh, Oswain stopped and threw off his pack.

'That's enough for today,' he said. 'We'd better set up camp before it gets dark.'

Peter and Sarah were mightily relieved. Their bodies ached all over and Sarah could hardly stand up for weariness.

Oswain looked at them with a rueful smile. 'I'm

sorry,' he said. 'We should have called a halt earlier. It's simply that I had hoped we would find her today.'

Sarah put her hand on his arm. 'It's not your fault,' she said. 'We wanted to find her, too. Anyway, let's get the tent up before we freeze to death. And you never know, she may turn up tonight.'

'You're right, Sarah,' Oswain replied. 'Come on, Peter, give me a hand with this lot, will you?'

The tent wasn't very large and they had to squeeze in a bit, but at least it would protect them from the cold of the mountains. They wrapped themselves in their travelling cloaks and blankets, ate some bread and cheese, then curled up and fell quickly to sleep.

It was Oswain who woke first. There was a strange sound outside. He felt in the darkness for Peter and Sarah and gave them a shake. It took some moments to rouse them.

'Wassermarra?' mumbled Peter. 'It's not morning already, is it?'

'No,' hissed Oswain. 'Listen. There's someone outside.'

At this Sarah sat bolt upright and brushed her head against the side of the tent.

'Is it the Ice Maiden?' she whispered excitedly.

'I don't know,' Oswain replied. 'Let's take a look.'

He leant over and undid the tent flap. All three poked their heads out at once.

It was still dark and the light of the stars shone coldly on the snow. All was quiet.

'There's no one . . .' began Peter.

'Quiet!' Oswain whispered. 'Look over there.'

The two children followed his gaze with wonderment. There in the darkness danced what looked like a cloud of brightly-lit diamonds, and it was coming towards where they lay. A crystal-like jingling filled the air and they felt their skins tingle with awe.

Suddenly, Peter pointed with his finger to their left. 'Look!' he gasped. 'There's another.'

'And another,' cried Sarah, glancing in the opposite direction.

In fact, there were soon dozens of these sparkling clouds dancing towards the tent. The air was filled with the silvery music of their presence and the whole place was bathed in a magical shimmering light.

'What are they?' gasped Peter.

'These, Peter, are the Naida,' Oswain replied in an awed voice.

'They're what I saw in my dream last night,' thought Sarah, and she shivered.

Chapter Seven

THE NAIDA

The three companions lay mesmerized at the door of their tent. Myriads of star-like Naida had gathered together into one vast cloud of shimmering, dazzling light. Their sound was like the tinkling of ten thousand tiny bells. All other thoughts and feelings were swamped by their unearthly presence.

There were no voices, but Oswain, Peter and Sarah each in their own way knew that the Naida were speaking to them. It happened first to Peter.

He felt himself running as fast as his legs would carry him. Some terrible urgency possessed him. His was a life or death mission. He had to get there in time. Over the open fields he ran, struggling up hills and stumbling down dales. His heart pounded fit to burst and his lungs cried out for rest. Sweat streamed from his brow and stung his eyes until he could scarcely see where he was going. Yet still he pressed on, driven by the urgent voice within. 'Faster, Peter. You must go faster or it will be too late.'

The sky grew sullen. Rain began to fall. The wind picked up, driving it hard into his face. Lightning flashed. Water streamed down the hills. He slipped and slithered, stumbled, fell, somehow struggled up. His legs felt like jelly but still he drove himself on, heedless of the pain.

Then he was through the storm and running down a long dusty road towards a stadium at the far end. He tried to sprint but his legs wouldn't respond. The voice urged him, wailing, crying for his help. He must make it in time.

With his legs buckling, he staggered into the stadium. It was empty. Then he knew he was too late. Despair, disappointment and failure overcame him. Slowly, he sank to the ground gasping and sobbing over his utter defeat. A terrible emptiness filled his heart, and then everything went dark.

Sarah was walking through a maze. In her hand she held a plan. Somewhere she could hear the loud ticking of a clock. She knew she had to reach the centre of the maze before the alarm rang.

The maze was large but Sarah followed the plan confidently, certain that she could work out a way through. In and out she wove, a left turn here, a right there, along here, through this gap. And all the while the ticking grew louder.

She was doing fine when, all of a sudden, a huge bird swept out of the sky, snatched the paper from her hand and flew off. Sarah was horrorstruck. Her mind went blank. Which way was she to go?

In blind panic she ran to the right. It was a dead end. So she turned and ran the other way. There were two exits. But she didn't know which was the right one. She stopped, clenched her fists and screwed her eyes up tight to overcome the panic. She must think. Try to remember the plan. The ticking was getting louder, and faster.

Sarah struggled to picture the map. It was so

difficult. Then, suddenly, she had it. As clear as day she could see it in her mind. She took the second exit and ran along to the right. It couldn't be far now. But the ticking was getting faster and faster. Hastily she took the left fork. She ran towards the last gap.

Too late! The alarm went off with a loud ringing. Sarah stopped in dismay. She had failed. Tears of frustration welled up in her eyes and slowly everything went black.

Oswain found himself walking the pleasant paths of the Great Forest. All of a sudden, through the trees, he spotted the figure of a white-robed woman. She was moving away from him. He began to follow her, curious to know who she was.

Without a backward glance she continued on her way until, at length, she left the forest and began to ascend into the mountains. Oswain hastened after her, but never seemed able to catch her up. All day he climbed but still she was ahead of him.

They were among the peaks where the snow carpeted the rocks. She moved with even greater ease but Oswain was soon struggling knee-deep through the snow. He was beginning to despair of reaching her.

Then, abruptly, she stopped and turned towards him. His heart leapt at her welcoming smile. He smiled back and made to shout a greeting. But before he could do so, some terrible blackness seemed to engulf the woman. Her face filled with horror as the darkness swallowed her up before his eyes.

Moments later, he lay alone and sad on the frozen wastes, utterly overcome by his loss. Sleep began to possess him.

But Oswain fought it.

'No!' he cried. 'I must know what has happened. Naida, you must tell me.' For Oswain realized that the Naida were the cause of his vision. He saw too that Peter and Sarah had fallen fast asleep under their spell.

In answer to his cry the bell-like tinkling changed in tone. It became a mournful sigh like the wind in the late autumn trees. Then it became an audible voice.

'Alas, alas, she is gone,' it sighed. 'They have taken her away and we are lost. Gone is the fair one of the mountains. We do not know what to do. Our power fades. Oh, help us, Oswain. Help us if you can.'

The Forest-King battled to stay awake in their presence.

'You must tell me more,' he insisted, 'before your presence overcomes me.'

Then in his mind Oswain saw Zarbid and the six black-robed priests climbing the slopes of the mountain. They reached the snow-line and came to a halt. He watched as the leader stripped off his dark robe revealing a tunic of white underneath.

The priests crouched behind nearby rocks as Zarbid advanced on to the snow. Suddenly, he fell and began to cry out in pain. Nobody moved to his aid. On and on he cried for help. Then Oswain saw the slender figure of the Ice Maiden walking towards the stricken man. He wanted to cry out that it was a trap, but knew it was no use now. She reached Zarbid and bent with kindness over him. He clutched at his leg.

To Oswain's horror, Zarbid slyly reached into his tunic and, with a sudden flick of his wrist, scattered a black powder on the snow around the Ice Maiden.

He scrambled to his feet and sprang away from her. An instant later the Ice Maiden found herself trapped in a circle of fire. Dismay clouded her features. The snow was melting all about her and within a minute she was standing upon the bare earth.

Zarbid stood at a distance replacing his cloak and watching the events with a satisfied leer on his face. As the flames died down the Ice Maiden gazed at him expectantly. He laughed out loud.

'No, I am not the one for whom you hoped,' Oswain heard him cackle. 'He's too late. You have transgressed your bounds before he has come, Ice Maiden. Now you are within *my* power!'

The Sorcerer slowly stretched forth his bony fingers and then suddenly scurried like a huge black spider to where the hapless Ice Maiden stood. He whirled around her, weaving a strange pattern with his hands. And as he did so, black gauze-like bandages swirled about her body. The Ice Maiden struggled to free herself, but within moments she was completely encased in a tight black cocoon. She fell helplessly to the ground and lay still.

Zarbid motioned to his cronies. They came running from behind the rocks with the empty coffin. Into it they dumped the Ice Maiden and then swiftly packed her around with snow and ice. The last thing Oswain saw was the lid being slammed shut and the priests carting off their prize down the mountain.

'She was deceived,' wailed the Naida. 'They trapped her with her own kindness . . . and her hope of your arrival. Now doom is written over the world. We can no longer defend these heights.'

Oswain fought back the bitter emotions which he felt.

'All is not lost,' he said thickly. 'My quest is not at an end just yet. Elmesh will help us.'

'Elmesh will help us,' echoed the Naida. Over and over again rang the refrain until Oswain slipped into as deep a sleep as his companions.

He awoke just as dawn was tinging the eastern sky. Though it was early summer, the weather was cold and bleak in these mountains. He shivered and woke the others.

'Did we dream what happened last night or was it real?' Peter enquired over breakfast. All three had recounted their experiences to one another as soon as they were awake enough to do so.

'The Naida are strange,' Oswain replied. 'You do not know altogether whether you are dreaming or not in their presence. But what we felt was the truth, I'm afraid.'

'You mean the Ice Maiden is captured?' Sarah said glumly. 'We really are too late?'

He nodded.

'So what do we do?' Peter asked. 'Should we go back and warn the others of war?'

Oswain shook his head.

'No, the innkeeper will see to that soon enough,' he replied. 'We go on. Elmesh told me to seek the Ice Maiden and that's what I intend to do.' He spoke determinedly and a fierce light was in his eye. 'Unless you two want to return,' he challenged.

'Oh, no. Not at all,' Peter replied hastily.

'I want us to rescue her,' Sarah answered simply. 'That's why Elmesh sent us and that's what we're to do, however dangerous it is.'

Oswain smiled and rose to his feet.

'Then we go at once to Traun,' he exclaimed. 'And woe betide those who performed this foul deed!'

Chapter Eight

THE SEARCH FOR KARADOR

Tarinda turned uneasily on her bed. She could hear her mother sobbing quietly behind a screen. It was now the third night since the fateful news of her father's capture and the Feast of Oris was only three days away.

She thought about the past two and a half days. Folk had searched high and low for news of Karador's whereabouts. Almost everyone had stopped their normal tasks to join in, though to her disgust the children had not been allowed to take part because of the dangers involved.

But it had been a discouraging task. There were literally miles of passages and caves running beneath the city of Traun and Zarbid might have hidden him almost anywhere. To make matters worse, the city was swarming with the dreaded Cryls, and they were watching every known entrance to the catacombs.

The only encouraging news was the rumour that Zarbid himself had been seen leaving the city. That could make rescuing Karador a bit easier—once they had found him. But everyone who had gone out had returned with the same glum story of a day's fruitless searching. It seemed hopeless.

Tarinda arose and went in to comfort her mother.

. . * . .

Tarinda awoke early the next morning. Pale light filtered down from the rim of the crater high above as she crept into the main chamber. All was quiet and she was alone.

At least, she thought she was. But just then she spotted the figures of Andrew and Tatters coming towards her.

'Hello,' whispered Andrew as they met. 'What are you doing up so early, Tarinda?'

'The same as you, I expect,' she replied guardedly. 'Where are you going?'

'Couldn't sleep,' he said. 'Thought I'd just take a walk around to stretch my legs.'

Tarinda glanced at Tatters. 'And I suppose you couldn't sleep either?' she challenged.

''Sright,' the dog replied.

'I don't believe either of you,' she said flatly. 'You're planning something and you haven't told me.'

Andrew smiled sheepishly.

'Sorry,' he said. 'You're right. We honestly couldn't sleep, but the real reason we're up is 'cos we want to do something about finding your dad. We started early so's the grown-ups wouldn't stop us.'

Tarinda was quiet and her lip quivered a bit. She was on the verge of tears. 'That's why I'm up, too,' she said. 'They won't let me go with them because they say it's too dangerous. But I don't care. I just want to find my dad.'

Tears rolled down her cheeks and she sniffed loudly. Andrew wasn't quite sure whether to put an arm round her or not. Tatters came to the rescue.

'Cheer up, Tarinda luv,' he said. 'We know 'ow you feel. That's why we want to 'elp. And as we've all got the same idea, we might as well join forces.' Then he added with a wink, 'And I've got an idea where we should start.'

Tarinda's glistening cheeks broke into a grateful smile. 'It's ever so kind of you both,' she said. 'And have you really got an idea, Tatters? Please tell me. I'll try anything to find my father.'

'Well, it's really very simple,' he answered, feeling rather pleased that he had cheered her up. 'I've run me feet off these past two days chasing up and down these 'ere catacombs. But there's one fing wot I've noticed, or rather wot I've not noticed.'

'Tell her what it is,' Andrew interrupted.

'Gimme half a chance and I will,' the dog retorted. 'It's just this. I ain't 'ad a single whiff of that Zarbid geezer anywhere. And I fink that if 'e'd been down these tunnels at all, I'd 'ave picked somefink up, 'cos 'e don't 'alf stink.'

'I don't understand how that helps us,' queried a puzzled Tarinda.

'Well don't yer see? If 'e ain't bin 'ere, then yer dad's not 'ere and we've bin looking for 'im in the wrong place. I reckon we got ter search in that temple, 'cos I bet that's where 'e's keeping 'im.'

'And that's where we were going this morning,' finished Andrew.

Tarinda's eyes were bright with excitement. 'Then what are we waiting for?' she exclaimed.

'Come on. Let's go while we've got the chance.'

The other two needed no second bidding and within a short while all three were standing on the hillside just beyond the city walls. They had come this way because they knew from what they'd heard that the Cryls would be watching the underground exits inside the city.

'Only one problem now,' observed Andrew. 'How do we get past the guards at the gates?'

They looked towards the entrance to the city. Although it was early in the morning a small queue of traders and their carts was already building up at the gates. Two guards were searching and questioning everyone.

'Only one way,' said Tatters. 'Create a diversion.'

He quickly outlined his plan to the other two.

Five minutes later a keen observer would have noticed two children who had joined the last cart in the queue gradually slipping along the line from one to another until they were almost at the front. There they chatted amiably to a man who had a barrow-load of apples, until a guard called 'next'. The trader pushed his cart forwards.

At that very moment, Tatters darted out of nowhere and began to snap at the guard's legs. The surprised soldier swore and tried to kick him out of the way. Tatters avoided the boot easily and attacked again, barking for all he was worth. Then the other guard joined in the fray and soon everyone was shouting and jeering at the comical sight of the two soldiers dancing about trying to keep their ankles from being nipped by this crazy dog.

All of a sudden, and before anyone could stop him, Tatters took a flying leap on to the apple-cart. Fruit flew wildly in all directions and created complete chaos. The grocer howled with rage and joined the soldiers in trying to catch the elusive mongrel before he did any more damage.

While all this commotion was taking place Andrew and Tarinda simply slipped quietly through the gates and scooted down the first street they could find. Tatters joined them about two minutes later, looking very pleased with himself.

'Cor, what a larf,' he chortled. 'I didn't 'alf make a mess back there. Could say I upset the apple cart!'

'Well done, Tatters,' Andrew laughed.

'Now let's get to the temple,' said Tarinda.

Since both she and Tatters knew the way it wasn't long before they were climbing the temple steps. Very few people were about and nobody took any notice of two children and a dog. They were soon inside the gloomy building and sneaking along the main corridor.

'It's down here,' said Tatters, showing them the way he had come before.

They reached the door to Zarbid's study. It was locked.

'Now what do we do?' Andrew sighed. 'We can hardly break the door down can we?'

'That's no problem,' said Tarinda with a smile. 'I can pick locks!'

So saying she took a pin from her hair and, while Andrew gazed dumbfounded, promptly began to work on the lock. A few moments later, there was a click and the door swung open.

'There!' said Tarinda proudly. 'Told you I could do it.'

'Fantastic!' Andrew marvelled.

They slipped into the study and closed the door behind them. There was very little furniture in the room, a desk and two chairs, and some shelves of books.

'Hm, not much here,' observed Tatters as he sniffed around.

'I'm going to try the drawers in this desk,' said Andrew. 'There might be a clue somewhere.'

He began to pull open the drawers. To his disappointment they were all empty.

'Don't think we've come to the right place somehow,' he muttered. 'I'll just try this last one and then we'd better get out of here before someone comes along.'

He gave the last drawer a pull. It was stiff and felt different. As he tugged it open he heard a scraping noise. A large stone slab had risen a few centimetres from the floor. They gathered round it excitedly.

'Reckon this is what we're looking for,' said Tatters. 'Give it a pull and let's see wot 'appens.'

Andrew and Tarinda gave the slab a heave and it swung back easily to reveal a flight of stone steps leading down to a wooden door.

'This has got to be it,' Andrew cried. 'Come on!'

They hastened down the stairs and tried the door. It wasn't locked. Cautiously, they swung it open and peered round. A dim light burned inside a large chamber. All around the room were strange objects whose purpose they could only guess at. It was an eerie place.

At one end of the chamber was a large black altar. They made towards it with care. All of a sudden, they heard a sound. They stood stock still. The noise came from somewhere on their left. The hair rising on her scalp, Tarinda slowly turned. She gasped, then cried out. 'Daddy! It's you!'

Andrew and Tatters spun round to see Tarinda running towards an iron-barred gate. Behind it stood the dark figure of a man whom they immediately took to be Karador.

'Tarinda!' he cried. 'Tarinda!'

They hugged each other through the bars, tears of joy and relief pouring down their faces.

'How did you ever get here, child?' he gasped.

'My new friends helped me,' she replied, and quickly introduced Andrew and Tatters. Karador was most interested to hear of how they had arrived.

'Elmesh be praised!' he exclaimed. 'But we must hurry. Can you open the lock?'

'There will be no need for that.' A hard grating voice from the doorway turned their blood to ice. All three turned at the sound and dismay filled their hearts. For there stood none other than the cloaked figure of Zarbid himself.

'Quick, run for it!' cried Karador.

'One each side of him,' Andrew shouted. 'He can't go both ways at once.'

The children darted for the door, only to find the way barred by several priests who were carrying a large box between them. There was no escape.

Tatters leapt at Zarbid and sank his fangs into the Sorcerer's arm. They fell struggling to the floor and Zarbid howled with rage and pain. Somehow he rolled clear and struggled to his feet. With a curse he drew out a black wand from his robe and pointed it at the dog.

He uttered a spell and there was a blinding flash. When it cleared, Tatters lay whimpering on the floor.

Andrew was horrified. 'Tatters! What's wrong?

74

What has he done to you?' he cried.

'It's me eyes,' groaned the dog. 'I can't see. 'E's gone and blinded me!'

Andrew rushed towards his companion.

'Stay where you are,' grated Zarbid. 'I haven't finished yet.'

He motioned to two of his cronies.

'Seize them!'

Andrew and Tarinda struggled to no avail as their arms were pinioned by their captors. Zarbid turned on the dog.

'Nobody attacks me,' he snarled. 'And no dogs may speak with people in this city. Dumb you shall be!' He uttered another spell and turned to one of his henchmen. 'Now throw this mongrel into the street. He can be food for whoever wants him.'

Andrew, Tarinda and Karador watched helplessly as the hapless dog was dragged away by the priest. Hot tears poured down Andrew's cheeks.

'Oh, Tatters,' he cried. 'What's going to happen to you?'

The dog merely whimpered in reply as a large tear rolled from his own soulful but now sightless eyes.

Once the dog had been removed it took Zarbid only minutes to find out the names of the children and they soon found themselves unceremoniously flung into the cell along with Karador. The coffin which the priests had been carrying was placed on the black altar.

The evil Sorcerer rubbed his gnarled hands with pleasure as he surveyed his handiwork.

'Hm, my plans are going even better than I anticipated,' he gloated. 'All I have to do now is sit and wait—until Oswain walks right into my trap!'

Chapter Nine

INSIDE THE CITY

While Andrew, Tarinda and Karador languished grief-stricken in Zarbid's underground gaol, Oswain, Peter and Sarah were heading down the mountainside towards the city. One day later, just as the rising sun was casting a pale pink glow on the high granite walls, they drew near to the gates of Traun.

'Well, here goes,' said Oswain as they joined the short queue of early morning traders.

'I feel scared,' Sarah confessed.

'Don't worry,' reassured her brother. 'They won't be expecting us and our disguises should be all right, anyway.'

'But I don't know anything about tinkering or whatever it's called,' she protested.

'Leave all the talking to me,' said Oswain. 'You're just my apprentices, remember?'

Sarah nodded and gulped. They were next in the queue.

But she need not have worried. Oswain easily convinced the guards and even unpacked some of his tools to demonstrate how they were used. And when they asked him about his sword, which he had thoughtfully sheathed in a rather tatty scabbard, he simply explained that the roads were dangerous and he thought it wise to carry one.

To their relief the guards were satisfied and soon the three companions were walking the unfamiliar cobbled streets of Traun.

'So this is where Surin lives,' murmured Oswain.

'It's a very hard place,' said Sarah. 'Nothing but grey stone. No trees or flowers.'

'Bit different from Elmar,' Peter commented.

'I think the way people build cities says what they're like inside themselves,' Sarah observed.

'Huh, doesn't say much for this lot then, does it?' Peter retorted.

Oswain smiled grimly. 'Surin is a hard king, living in a hard land and worshipping harsh gods. He has little time for beauty as you and I think of it,' he said. 'Conquest and war is what gives him most pleasure.'

'Ugh!' said Sarah. 'Perhaps that's why all these people look so miserable.'

The city was becoming steadily busier as they wandered through the streets. Shops and stalls were opening. Horses and carts were clattering along the cobbles to deliver their wares. It wasn't long before the trio were well caught up in the noisy throng of workers and shoppers going about their daily business.

'Just what we needed,' said Oswain. 'We're less conspicuous like this.'

'I'm getting hungry,' Peter announced. 'How about some breakfast?'

'Good idea,' Oswain agreed. 'Let's try that inn over there.'

He indicated a faded wood-fronted building on a

corner from which wafted the pleasant aroma of frying bacon and fresh-baked bread.

The inn was a crowded, noisy affair with bright sunlight streaming through the smoke-laden atmosphere and a rich variety of smells to make the mouth water. The three friends managed with difficulty to find a table in a corner by the window.

'I'll go and order some food,' said Oswain. 'I shouldn't be long. But keep your eyes open for trouble, and don't move from here.'

With that he disappeared into the smoke and began to press through the crowd towards the busy innkeeper.

Sarah smiled at her brother. 'You know, this is really rather cosy,' she said. 'Better than being stuck on top of a freezing mountain.'

'I think I'd be happier there,' Peter replied, his eyes darting around warily. Some of the characters looked unsavoury. 'Don't forget we're right under the noses of our enemies.'

'Do you think we'll be able to find the Ice Maiden?' Sarah asked. 'I haven't a clue where to start.'

'Oswain will have some ideas, you'll see,' her brother reassured her. 'I wonder what he's ordered for breakfast. I'm starving.'

'He's taking his time, isn't he?'

'Lot of people here. Never get quick service in a pub,' Peter answered with the air of one who knows.

They waited a few more minutes but still Oswain didn't return. Sarah was growing impatient. 'I think we should go and look for him,' she said. 'I don't like it.'

'Don't worry,' her brother replied. 'And remember he told us to stay here.'

Reluctantly, Sarah agreed and they continued to wait. But there was still no sign of Oswain. The inn began to empty. Suddenly, they realized that there were only a few occupants left—and Oswain was not among them.

Peter looked grimly at his sister. 'I think you're right, Sarah. Something has happened to Oswain. Come on. Let's get out of here quick!'

'Oh dear,' wailed Sarah. 'Now what are we going to do?'

· · * · ·

Tatters sat all day on the steps of the temple pining for his master. Every so often he let out a long, mournful howl. He didn't know why. It was just something deep inside him which welled up like a sad song that had to be sung.

He had no idea of how long he sat there. People came and went; he could smell their scent and hear their footsteps and the sound of their voices. The sun felt warm on his coat for a while but it passed and later the air grew chilly. Perhaps it was nearly night. He was desperately thirsty but even thirst would not persuade him to break his lonely vigil. The faithful dog knew that he would probably sit there until he died.

Many hours passed. Night came and the city slept. Yet still that strange loyalty of a dog for his master held Tatters bound to the spot.

Then, in the early hours of the morning something happened which was to change everything. Tatters heard a voice which he recognized. It was

Hercules, the leader of the hounds.

'I say, hello there, old chap. It's you again, isn't it? What are you doing here at this hour?'

Tatters croaked painfully in reply. Thankfully, he found he could still speak in dog language, even though he had lost his human tongue. "Erc, it's you, ain't it? Listen, I'm in trouble, mate. Terrible trouble.'

The hound was right by his side and pushed a comforting wet nose against his fur. 'What is it, old friend? What's happened to you?' he asked in a voice full of concern.

With great difficulty Tatters told his tale. 'And now I'm blind, and I can't talk to 'umans, and me master's in gaol,' he finished woefully. 'What am I gonna do, 'Erc?' With a long whimpering moan he drooped his head to the ground.

The hound was silent for a long while. 'I would like to tear that Zarbid to shreds,' he growled angrily. 'But that's no answer at the moment. And nor is you sitting here pining, old chum. I know how you feel and all that, but what we need is action. We must get you back to Clea as soon as possible.'

'But I can't tell 'er nuffink, can I?' Tatters protested.

'No, but between us we can show someone the way back here,' Hercules replied. 'Come on. It's your only chance. Let me be your eyes and I'll show you the way.'

Reluctantly Tatters agreed and so, after lapping some much needed water from a horse-trough by the roadside, they set off together.

'What about them wild-cats?' Tatters asked, after a while.

'Never fear, old chap. They're terrified of me. One of their leaders attacked me once. Nobody ever tried it since!' the hound replied. 'Anyway, I'm taking you a different route. There's a way into the catacombs not far from here. Don't let strangers use it as a rule, but this is an emergency.'

Before very long the two dogs came to a blind alley. Hercules led Tatters to the far end. By the side of a house was an old set of stone steps which led down to a broken door at the bottom.

'We're in a disused cellar,' Hercules explained as he led his companion through the door. 'We found it some years ago. There's a hole in the corner which leads into a tunnel. It'll take us to the main catacombs where we can find our way back to the volcano and to your friends. Just follow me.'

They seemed to pad for miles along the under-ground corridors but Tatters could smell that people had been here recently and knew that Hercules was taking him in the right direction. Not that he had any worries about the hound; he was proving to be a real friend in time of need. Tatters could feel his spirits rising again.

'Nearly there, old bean,' said Hercules. 'Just round this bend and on the left.'

Moments later they emerged from the catacombs and passed unnoticed into the bustling slave commune.

'Better find Clea,' said Tatters. 'Wears a red cloak. Usually somewhere in the middle of fings.'

'Hm, awful lot of people about,' Hercules answered. 'Could take us ages.'

But at that moment Tatters heard someone call his name. He didn't recognize the voice.

'Tatters, its me, Danir!' the voice called again.

'We've been looking for you everywhere. Where have you been? And where are Andrew and Tarinda?'

The blind dog turned his head in the direction of the voice and whimpered.

'What's that?' said Danir. 'I can't understand you.'

Tatters barked, then tried to lead Danir towards the tunnel entrance. But he wouldn't follow. Hercules joined in and began to bay loudly. It was no use.

'I don't know what's up with you,' exclaimed Danir in exasperation. 'But you obviously haven't got the children with you. You'd better come with me to find Clea, and quick.'

'Thank goodness for that,' sighed Hercules. 'If only I hadn't lost my human voice all those years ago . . .'

Danir shot off as fast as his legs could carry him, leaving the dogs to follow as best they could. It took only minutes to find Clea. Her face looked dreadfully drawn but she was on her feet the instant she saw Tatters.

'What's happened?' she asked the dog. 'Where are the children?'

Tatters tried to communicate with her. He rubbed himself against her leg and whimpered, then lifted a paw to his face. She stooped and took his head between her hands.

'Why what is it, Tatters?' she asked gently.

By way of answer, the dog again wiped a paw across his face and whined. Clea gazed intently at him then turned her head grim-faced towards Danir who stood nearby.

'This dog is blind,' she said quietly. 'Some terrible evil has befallen him.' She addressed the dog. 'Can you speak, Tatters?'

He barked. She nodded with understanding then rose to her feet.

'I believe they've encountered Zarbid. Somehow Tatters has escaped. But not Tarinda nor Andrew.' Clea's voice trembled. 'What are we going to do, Danir?'

At that moment, Hercules seized her robe between his teeth and began to yank on it. She got the message at once.

'They know where they are,' she gasped. 'They want us to follow.'

'I'll call Haemor,' said Danir. 'Leave it to us, Clea. We'll go with them.'

She tried to protest but Danir insisted that she remain behind. 'The people need you,' he argued. 'You must lead them at this time. Trust us. We'll do all we can to rescue the children.'

'I think the message has got through, old boy,' drawled Hercules.

'Baht time, too,' Tatters answered. "Umans is so fick sometimes!'

Moments later and the giant Haemor was with them. He carried a fearsome double-bladed axe in his hand. Danir had donned a short sword and carried a lethal-looking club.

'We're ready,' announced the latter.

'Elmesh be with you,' whispered Clea. 'All depends upon you.'

Haemor addressed Hercules, who stood waiting expectantly. 'Lead the way, my fine friend,' he bellowed. 'Let's be finding them, then.'

And with that they were off, Hercules in front, followed by Danir and Haemor with Tatters in his arms. Clea watched them go. She knew the fate of her husband and her daughter hung upon their success.

Chapter Ten

BREAKOUT!

Hercules sped down the tunnel, weaving his way confidently through the various twists and turns until they came at length to the old basement cellar in the centre of the city. There he halted.

'Phew! That was a good run,' laughed the agile Danir.

Haemor wasn't so sure. He was looking very red-faced. 'It's all right for featherweights like you,' he puffed. 'But not for the likes of me—and don't forget I've got Tatters.' He looked around. 'Anyway, where are we?'

'Somewhere inside the city, that's for sure,' Danir replied. 'I didn't know this entrance existed. Could be useful.'

'Hm, well we'd better let the dog lead on,' Haemor answered. 'And keep your eyes open for Cryls.' He addressed Hercules who looked up at him alertly. 'Well done, my friend. Now where do we go from here? But wherever it is, let's go a bit slower, if you don't mind!'

Hercules gave a bark to let him know that he had understood, then made for the door and up the steps into the alley.

It took them some little while to get within sight of the temple. On several occasions they had to double back on their tracks because they had spotted Cryls keeping a lookout on street corners. It would not do for them to raise the alarm.

'Have we got to get into the temple?' Danir asked when they were only one block away. Tatters growled what he hoped would sound like 'yes'.

Haemor glanced around. 'Not too many people about. We'd best make a run for the entrance and hope nobody spots us,' he said.

'All right, but I think one at a time,' suggested Danir. He addressed Hercules. 'You go first. Give us a bark if it looks all clear.'

This way all four gained the temple portals without any mishap. Haemor put Tatters down and they began to creep warily down the central corridor. Hercules went on ahead. Suddenly, he came hurtling back.

'Trouble,' snapped Danir. 'Quick, down here.'

They threw themselves into the shadows of a side passage just in time. None other than Zarbid was hastening past. All four held their breaths and waited. To their horror the Sorcerer came to a halt. He sniffed, and glanced suspiciously in their direction. Then he took a step.

Tatters reacted instantly. Even though he couldn't see where he was going he bounded towards the sound made by the Sorcerer.

Zarbid laughed out loud when he saw him. 'Oh, it's you is it, you worthless cur. The wild-cats not got you yet? Never mind, they will. It's no use hanging around here. You're as good as dead!'

And with that the Sorcerer went on his way.

'Phew! That was close,' breathed Haemor. 'Well

done, Tatters.'

'Yes,' agreed Danir. 'And that's Zarbid out of the way too. At least for the moment.'

Tatters, feeling very pleased with himself, sniffed around and then led the way until they came to the door of Zarbid's study. It was locked.

'What do you think?' asked Danir doubtfully, with a glance over his shoulder.

By way of reply the giant Haemor smiled grimly. Without a word he swung back his axe and brought it down with a loud crash against the lock. The wood splintered and the door swung open under the weight of the blow. Moments later they were inside the study.

Tatters shot at once across to the desk, bumping his nose in his haste, and began to tug on the bottom drawer with his teeth. The others watched him curiously.

'He must want us to look in there,' said Danir. He pulled the stiff drawer open. 'Hm, nothing in it,' he observed. 'I wonder why Tatters . . .?'

'Wait,' interrupted Haemor. 'What was that scraping?'

'Over there somewhere, 'Erc,' Tatters whuffed to the hound. 'Can't remember exactly where it is but there's a slab in the floor that oughta be open a bit.'

'I see it,' Hercules answered, and bounded across to the trapdoor.

'Well, I'll be blowed!' exclaimed Haemor. 'Look at this, Danir.'

He bent and swung the slab open to reveal the steps. Nobody needed a second bidding. All four piled down to the door at the bottom.

'Watch out for guards,' cautioned Danir.

Haemor slowly eased the door open. The room

seemed to be empty.

'All clear,' he hissed.

They looked around the gloomy underground lair. Suddenly, there was a cry.

'Haemor! Danir! Over here.'

Karador stood at the bars of his cell beckoning urgently with his hand. Behind him stood Tarinda and Andrew.

The two men, beaming all over their faces, rushed across to their leader.

'How did you find us?' gasped Karador.

Haemor pointed to the two dogs.

Andrew recognized Tatters at once.

'Tatters, it's you,' he cried. 'You're alive!'

The dog bounded towards the sound of his master's voice. Andrew flung his arms around him through the bars and hugged him tightly. Tears of relief poured down his face.

'I'm so glad you're here,' he sobbed.

Karador addressed Haemor. 'Can you get us out of here, my friend?'

The red-haired giant eyed the bars with scorn.

'Stand clear, all of you,' he ordered.

He took a step back then, with a roar, smashed the sole of his boot against the lock. It remained firm. Twice more he repeated the action, then rattled the door. It was now very loose. He stepped back a few paces, paused, and then hurled his whole weight against the bars. There was a squeal of tortured metal and the gate swung open with a loud clang.

Haemor, puffing and panting, beamed down from his flushed face at his amazed friends. Karador laughed loudly.

'I'm truly glad you're on our side, that's all!' he

said. 'Now come on, let's get out of here while we can.'

'But what are we going to do about the Ice Maiden?' Andrew asked. From Zarbid's conversations with his cronies they had worked out who was in the coffin.

Karador eyed the casket doubtfully.

'I don't know,' he said. 'We can't take it with us now and we don't even know if she's alive. I'm not sure what we should do.'

'We must get out of here at once,' urged Haemor. 'There's no time to lose.' He glanced across at Danir who was rummaging through some scrolls on a desk. 'What are you doing, Danir?' he bellowed. 'This is no time for reading. Come on!'

Danir ignored him. He was frowning over a piece of parchment in his hand. Suddenly his face lit up.

'This is it!' he cried. 'Just what I was looking for.'

He handed the parchment to Karador.

'It's the document that Balgus signed,' he explained. 'Tatters told us about it. If we can get this to Surin somehow then Balgus and Zarbid are finished.'

Karador glanced down at the scroll.

'You're right,' he said fiercely. 'Well found, Danir.' He glanced at the impatient Haemor and grinned. 'Now, let's be on our way.'

They were halfway up the steps when trouble struck. Danir was in front and almost ran headlong into three men armed with drawn swords.

'Cryls!' he gasped.

Quick as a flash he swung his club up to protect himself from a lethal swordstroke and skilfully succeeded in disarming one of the men at the same time. In a moment Haemor was by his side and his broad axe soon proved more than a match for the swordsmen. All three fled for their lives.

'Run for it,' cried Karador. 'They'll raise the alarm in no time.'

Haemor grabbed Tatters, and with Karador leading they dashed through the temple and out on to the steps. At that very moment, a band of Cryls burst from a side street on the left.

'This way,' shouted Karador, pointing in the opposite direction.

They poured down the steps and into a long alley, rapidly pursued by the Cryls who had now seen them.

But Karador knew these streets like the back of his hand and before long they had lost their pursuers in a maze of narrow passageways. Abruptly, he stopped by the door of a small house.

'In here,' he panted. 'Quickly!'

He ushered them into a narrow hallway.

'Up those stairs,' he commanded as he closed the door behind them.

They found themselves in a bare room scarcely four metres square. Karador threw himself flat against the wall and glanced cautiously out of the grimy window. They were just in time; a band of Cryls came running down the street only moments later. They ran on past the house.

'We're safe for the moment,' puffed the slave leader. 'But we'll have to lie low until things quieten down a bit.'

He laughed, then walked across the room with arms outstretched to hug Haemor and Danir in turn.

'Well done, my friends,' he said in a voice full of appreciation. 'You have saved my life and probably that of Tarinda and her friend too. I shall never forget your bravery.'

'We'd never have done it without the help of these two dogs,' Danir pointed out.

Karador smiled down at them.

'I don't know if you understand me or not,' he said. 'But I want to thank you for your courage. Know that Karador will never forget you either.'

Both Tatters and Hercules barked to let him know that they had understood. He laughed.

At that moment, Andrew gave a loud gasp. He was peering through the window. Karador shot to his side.

'What is it, Andrew?' he demanded.

'I don't believe it,' answered the boy in a strained voice. He pointed with a shaking finger. 'Those two there. That's my brother and my sister!'

Chapter Eleven

WHAT HAPPENED
TO OSWAIN

Oswain never knew what hit him. Having jostled his way through the crowd to the innkeeper he had just ordered breakfast when the blow fell on the back of his head. He never felt the rough hands seize his falling body and hustle him away, never observed the innkeeper discreetly turning his attention to other customers nor those nearby choosing not to notice what had happened. This was Traun and it was better not to get involved.

He came round to find himself lying on a dirt floor in a small room. Something was tugging at his leg. He struggled to focus his eyes. Before him stood five fierce-looking brigands. Another was trying to wrench off one of his boots. Instinctively, Oswain's hand flew to his sword, but it was gone, as was his cloak and all his other possessions, including his ring. In fact, the leader of the gang was holding the latter up to the light at that very moment.

Oswain lashed out at the thug who was trying to steal his boots. Immediately, several of the others fell upon him and pinned him to the ground. He struggled helplessly against the overwhelming odds. One of them had him by the throat.

But just then the door flew open with a loud crash.

'Cryls! Run for it!' cried a hoarse voice.

The effect was electric. In moments the gangsters had fled the room leaving Oswain lying dazed on the floor. He struggled to his feet, feeling ruefully grateful that he had at least still got his boots. But then the seriousness of the situation hit him. He had been robbed of everything he possessed and he had lost Peter and Sarah in the bargain. They might be in grave danger themselves. He knew he must try to find them as soon as possible.

But before he could do anything further the door flew open once more. Oswain thought for a moment that the brigands had returned to finish the job. He made ready to fight. Instead, he was confronted by a stern-looking officer dressed in black and carrying a drawn sword. Several others were behind him. He glanced quickly around the room then addressed Oswain in clipped tones.

'Who are you, stranger? Your name and business, if you please.'

Oswain's heart sank. These were the feared Cryls. He was in just as much danger now as he had been a few moments before. He tried stalling.

'Thank goodness you arrived,' he replied with feigned gratitude. 'I'm a visitor to this city and I've just been attacked by thieves. You've probably saved my life. Alas, I have lost everything else.'

The Cryl looked him over.

'You may think yourself fortunate, then,' he snapped coldly. 'But you haven't answered my question. What is your name and your business in this city?'

Oswain hesitated.

It was enough for the suspicious Cryl. He called to his men behind him. 'This man could be the one we're looking for. Arrest him and take him to Balgus.'

Before Oswain could so much as move he was surrounded by four armed Cryls. He knew it would be foolish to resist so he remained impassive as they bound his wrists and led him away. He only hoped he could find some way of escape later.

·   ·   *   ·   ·

Zarbid was discussing the plans for war with Surin when one of the priests sent a message that he was urgently needed outside. The Sorcerer immediately assumed that Oswain had been seen, or better still captured. He had already alerted Balgus and his Cryls to be on the lookout for the ruler of the Great Forest whom he expected to slip into the city any day. But when instead he was told that Karador had escaped his hope turned to fury. In great haste he excused himself from Surin in order to return to the temple.

'By the gods, I would like to know how this was done,' he fumed as he surveyed the scene. Only his most trusted servants knew of this underground chamber and they would not have betrayed anything.

To his relief the Ice Maiden was still lying unconscious in the casket on the altar. 'At least I still have the means to trap Oswain,' he thought. But his comfort was short-lived. He suddenly noticed that all his parchments had been rifled. With a cry of rage he ran to the desk and searched desperately through them. There was no sign of the document which Balgus had signed.

'Curses,' he spat. 'I must get that scroll back or I'm finished.' His suspicious mind wondered whether Balgus himself had obtained it. Had it already reached Surin?

His thoughts were interrupted by a call from one of his servants. Balgus was coming to see him. Grim-faced, Zarbid hastened up the stairs back to his study and closed the secret passageway. He composed himself to meet the head of the Cryls.

Balgus looked troubled as he strode into the study. He refused to sit down and paced the room agitatedly. 'How in the name of Damil did he escape?' Balgus exclaimed. 'I thought you had him secure.'

'So I did,' snapped the Sorcerer. 'Almost no one else knew of his whereabouts, not even you.'

'That's hardly surprising seeing you intended to blackmail me,' sneered Balgus. 'And where has it got you? You've lost me Karador. What am I supposed to say to the king? It's the Feast tomorrow. I'm ruined if I don't produce the prisoner.' He turned angrily and faced Zarbid across the desk. 'I want that scroll I signed,' he growled. 'Give it to me or I'll break your neck.'

Zarbid ignored the threat and eyed him shrewdly.

'Then you do not have the scroll already?' he ventured.

'No, of course I don't,' snapped Balgus. 'How could I? Why?'

'The scroll has gone,' Zarbid said flatly.

Balgus stared aghast. 'Then I'm a dead man,' he whispered hoarsely. 'Once Surin gets hold of . . . .'

'Bah!' interrupted Zarbid. 'Stop snivelling about your own fate. What about me? If it falls into Surin's hands it will hardly take him long to work out my part in all this. He's no fool.'

'Then we must flee the city at once,' cried Balgus. 'Before it's too late.'

'Fool, we would be hunted down like animals if we did that,' Zarbid hissed. 'No, we will stick to the plan but we must act more swiftly than I intended. Surin must die as soon as . . . .'

He was interrupted just then by one of the Cryls bursting into the room. He addressed Balgus.

'Beg pardon, sir, but you did say to call you as soon as there was news. We have someone we think you may be looking for.'

Balgus smirked. 'Our problems may be solved after all,' he said smugly. 'Bring him in,' he commanded the Cryl.

Moments later, Oswain was marched into the room. Balgus' face clouded with disappointment. He had hoped it would be Karador standing before them, not this stranger.

But Zarbid was delighted. He recognized at once who it was.

'So, you decided to pay us a visit, King Oswain?' he sneered. 'Couldn't resist the attractive bait I laid, eh? I thought not. And so easily caught, too. So much for your worthless god!'

Oswain remained impassive.

'Nothing to say, I suppose?' the Sorcerer continued. 'No matter. You are in our power and that is sufficient for the moment.' He turned to Balgus. 'Your men have done well, Balgus; exceedingly well if I may say so. That certainly sweetens the bitter pill we've swallowed this day, eh?'

Balgus wasn't so sure. He looked doubtfully at Oswain.

'Don't you realize?' insisted Zarbid. 'We have in our grasp the one man who might have provided some opposition to our invasion of the South. Without him they have nothing. They are powerless to stop us!' He addressed Oswain. 'Oh yes, and I have the Ice Maiden, too,' he said. 'I have kept her alive just so that you might be present to watch her death —before you die yourself!'

'You will not succeed,' Oswain replied quietly. 'Elmesh will deliver us from your evil plans.' Even though Zarbid appeared to hold all the cards, Oswain was not prepared to lose hope that easily.

Zarbid laughed mockingly. 'Elmesh will deliver us,' he mimicked. 'Pah, you are pathetic, Oswain. Your god is nothing compared to the threefold might of Igur, Damil and Oris. We will sweep your whole nation to its doom and your Elmesh will become nothing but a fading memory.'

Oswain said nothing. Time would tell.

Zarbid motioned to the Cryls. 'Take him away to Surin. No, wait.' He looked slyly at Balgus. 'Take him out to the court of the gods. Lock him in the cell by the altar instead. I will inform Surin myself. And load him with chains. I want there to be no possibility of escape.'

As soon as they had left the room Zarbid seized Balgus by the tunic. 'Now listen,' he hissed. 'This is our best chance. We've got to strike tonight. Now, I have a plan . . . .'

Two hours later Zarbid visited King Surin at the palace. He was accompanied by Murg, the commander of the army, to whom he had already spoken.

97

'Good news, Sire,' beamed the Sorcerer as he entered the state room.

Surin looked up from his affairs. 'Well go on then. What is it?' he demanded.

'We have captured Oswain, your Majesty,' answered the Sorcerer.

Surin rose slowly to his feet and smiled broadly.

'You have captured Oswain?' he echoed. 'This is indeed good news to my ears. You have done excellently, Zarbid. First the Ice Maiden and now Oswain. Excellent!'

Zarbid bowed. 'Thank you, Sire,' he replied smoothly.

'Well, where is he?' the King demanded. 'I want to see him. Do you have him outside, Murg?'

'I have him in the temple,' Zarbid answered. 'I did not see fit to bring one such as him into your royal presence. He is of the lower kind, your Majesty; not worthy of a royal court. Thus I have treated him.'

Surin frowned. 'But not too bad for your temple? You behave strangely, Zarbid.'

'It was only out of consideration for your Majesty,' replied the Sorcerer.

'Very well, if you say so. But I will see him soon. I have things to say to that stealer of my daughter!'

'Yes, of course, Sire,' Zarbid acknowledged. At that point he gave Murg a surreptitious glance. The soldier stepped forward.

'If it please you, your Majesty,' he began. 'Now that the way is open for us to attack the South, may I suggest that we do not delay to do so? The troops are ready and restless for battle.'

'Yes, of course,' agreed Surin. He smacked his fist into the palm of his hand. 'I too am ready for war.

My revenge is long overdue. We march tomorrow or the day after.'

'May I recommend a greater haste than that,' put in Zarbid. 'Tomorrow is the Feast of Oris and not a good day to march out the men. And if you keep them in the city they will be too drunk to march on the following day.'

'Not only that,' added Murg, who had been briefed beforehand, 'but the longer we delay the more it allows time for the forces of the South to organize their defences.'

'But we will sweep them down, anyway,' Surin objected. 'They will never stand before our forces.'

'True, but the quicker the better,' Murg insisted. 'It will keep the bankers happy and mean a smaller loss of troops for us.'

'And if I may say so, Sire,' said Zarbid, looking him straight in the eye, 'I desire you to have the satisfaction of your revenge as soon as possible. How long you have waited, your Majesty. How the yearning has festered in your heart. You have been greatly insulted. Let it not ever be said that Surin of Traun delayed to exact vengeance when he had the opportunity. After all,' he added, 'others might seek to take advantage of such leniency.'

'Very well,' agreed Surin. 'It is no matter to me when we march. How soon can we be ready?'

'Within the hour,' Murg replied promptly. 'We have been preparing for days.'

Surin raised his eyebrows. 'Hm, that is soon,' he remarked. 'But nonetheless efficient and I like to lead a well-disciplined army. But it gives me little time to prepare myself for travel.'

At this point, Zarbid approached the king and led him by the arm to one side. 'Ah, if I might say, your

Majesty, it is not actually necessary for you to lead the army out yourself today. Murg can do that. They will encamp but a few leagues before nightfall and it would be an easy matter for you to join them on fast horseback tomorrow.'

'But why?' queried Surin.

'Have you forgotten, Sire, it is the Feast of Oris tomorrow. Prudent it may be to set the army on its way today, but you must be present at the sacrifices. The people expect it, as do the gods —and we need their favour for the war.'

Surin hesitated. The Sorcerer continued: 'May I recommend, Sire, that you give dignity to the parade by taking the salute at the city gates? There will be no loss of face in that. Indeed, it will give the men confidence to think that you can join them at your convenience.'

'Very well,' agreed the king. 'It is not my usual custom. Nevertheless, I will do as you say. It will not do for me to be absent from the feast. Your words have the appearance of wisdom, Zarbid.'

Zarbid bowed. 'One other matter, your Majesty. As you will then be occupied for the rest of today, may I suggest that you visit the prisoner Oswain after nightfall, once the army is on its way?'

Surin consented and with that the interview was over.

So it was that within a short while the whole city was suddenly abuzz with the unexpected news that the army was about to march to war. Crowds gathered quickly to watch the parade.

Surin sat erect and proud upon his horse as his troops paraded past him and through the city gates. Company after company of cavalry each with its banners unfurled and trumpets sounding trotted over the cobbles to the cheers of the people. They were followed by wagons laden with provisions and weapons, and craftsmen of all kinds who would build bridges, make battering rams and huge mangonels—giant catapults that could hurl rocks over vast distances. Behind them came scores of heavily-armed infantrymen.

Kraan boasted one of the most powerful armies in living memory. Not once had they lost a battle under the brilliant and ruthless leadership of their warrior-king. Many had cause to fear them. More than that, it was known that their gods were strong. Strange tales abounded of armies who had been put to flight by fearsome creatures or dread winds conjured up by the priests of Kraan.

Surin felt confident. The very sight of his men in battle array stirred the blood-lust within him. He looked forward to conquering at last the land which had so long withstood his power. And he vowed he would kill his disowned daughter, Princess Alena, with his own bare hands. Then his revenge would be complete!

Chapter Twelve

HERCULES FOLLOWS THE SCENT

Andrew stared flabbergasted through the window. There was no doubt about the identity of the boy and girl walking slowly up the street; they were Peter and Sarah, his own brother and sister! But how on earth did they get here?

He wasted no more time in finding out. Before Karador or anyone else could counsel caution he dashed out of the room and thundered down the stairs to the front door. The quick-witted Danir was right behind him but only just managed to prevent him from flinging the door wide open and running straight out on to the street.

'Easy does it, Andrew,' he cautioned. 'You never know if Cryls are watching. Let me look first.'

Reluctantly Andrew agreed and stood back while Danir eased open the door and glanced quickly up and down the street. There appeared to be no one else about except the two children. He held the door just slightly ajar and waited. They had almost reached the house.

'Psst,' he hissed just as they drew level. 'Peter! Over here. You too, Sarah.'

At the mention of their names the children

stopped dead.

'Is that you, Oswain?' Peter whispered to the figure crouched behind the door.

'No, it's not,' Danir answered. 'But I am a friend and I've got someone here who wants to meet you. Come inside quickly if the coast is clear.'

The children hesitated. 'It may be a trap,' Peter warned his sister. 'Get ready to run.'

'Open the door wide so that we can see you,' Sarah insisted.

'All right,' Danir agreed. 'But you're in for a surprise so don't make a sound.'

With that, he flung the door open to reveal both himself and Andrew.

Peter and Sarah's eyes nearly popped out of their heads when they saw their brother. Sarah's hand flew to her mouth to stifle her cry of surprise.

'Get inside quick!' Danir urged.

They were in like a shot and, while Danir closed the door, all three flung their arms around each other to incredulous cries of, 'What are you doing here?'

'We'd better all go upstairs,' said Danir. 'It's safer there. And we must let Karador know what's happening.'

A delighted Tatters was the first to greet Peter and Sarah. Even though he couldn't see them he still managed a flying leap straight into Sarah's arms. She fell back laughing.

'Tatters, you're here, too!' she gasped. 'This is fantastic!'

Both she and Peter bent down to fondle the excited dog. Karador looked on with an amused smile. 'We're becoming quite a party,' he said. 'You had better introduce your brother and sister, Andrew.'

The boy nodded and, when he had got Peter and Sarah's attention, proudly presented to them Karador, Tarinda, Haemor, Danir and Hercules. He then explained all that had happened to him and Tatters since they had fallen into this realm, including how Tatters had been given the gift of human speech, but then had been struck dumb and blinded by Zarbid.

Sarah glowered when she heard this. 'How could anyone be so wicked?' she exclaimed. She knelt down and put her arms around the dog. 'Poor Tatters! What has he done to you?' she commiserated.

Tatters responded with a plaintive whine.

'Anyway, that's it, really,' Andrew finished. 'Now you'd better tell us your story.'

Peter began with how they had arrived in the Tower of Visions and then told of their journey to Traun and of their meeting with the Naida.

Karador listened to their story with great interest and asked many probing questions about Oswain and his mission. At length he seemed satisfied. He addressed Peter and Sarah.

'What the Naida have told you is true,' he said. 'Zarbid does have the Ice Maiden. She is held captive in his lair, though I do not know if she still lives. Either way, the news is grave for the South, for Surin will surely go to war against them.'

'And if not he, then certainly Zarbid will,' interjected Danir. 'Don't forget his plot to kill Surin.'

'I am but the leader of a slave band,' Karador continued. 'I seek only to rescue people who are victims of cruelty and injustice. We have little interest in kings and the fate of other nations. But your

Oswain serves Elmesh even as we do, and for that alone we will gladly help you in your task.'

Sarah and Peter smiled gratefully.

'Thank you,' said Sarah.

Karador rose to his feet. 'Our first task must be to find Oswain. It may be that he has stumbled upon something, or perhaps has fallen already into the hands of the Cryls. We must find out.' He turned to Danir. 'It's time we got out of here. Check that it's safe. The Cryls should have moved on by now.'

Danir left the room.

'We'll start at *The Lingal*,' he said. 'We should pick up some rumours there.'

Danir confirmed that the coast was clear so, with Karador leading, the party slipped into the maze of narrow streets which marked the poorest part of the city.

They came after a while to an unsavoury looking inn called *The Lingal*.

'No use us all going in,' advised Haemor. 'That'll raise too many suspicions.'

'Agreed,' said Karador. 'You and Danir go and see what you can pick up. We'll wait here and keep watch.'

The remainder of the party crouched behind a low wall opposite as the two men entered the inn. Nothing happened for a long time except for an occasional customer entering or leaving.

They were just beginning to tire of waiting when the door of the inn crashed open and a bunch of rowdy, rough-looking men staggered noisily on to the street. Peter gave a start.

'Look!' he cried. 'One of them's wearing Oswain's cloak.'

Karador was at his side in an instant.

'Are you sure?' he demanded.

'Yes, Peter's right,' Sarah confirmed.

'That's Brond and his gang,' said Karador. 'Worthless thieves all of them. Stay here and I'll see what he's been up to.'

They watched as Karador sauntered over to the gang leader and began to talk with him. It was too far away to hear what they were saying but all of a sudden the drunken Brond gave Karador an angry shove. The gang closed in around him.

At once, Hercules shot from his hiding place and bounded across to Karador's side. He bared his teeth and began to bark at the mob. The noise quickly attracted the attention of Haemor and Danir. They burst out of the inn to see what all the commotion was about. Haemor let out an angry cry when he spotted the gang. His hand flashed to his belt.

One look at the fiery giant wielding his huge battle-axe was enough for the cowardly thugs and they fled for their lives. But Karador was too quick for the leader. With a flying dive he brought him crashing to the ground and leapt upon him.

'That's as far as you go, Brond,' he cried. 'Now, you tell me where you stole this cloak or I'll get Haemor to break every bone in your body!'

'What's it to you, Karador?' the brigand gasped. 'We've all got to make a living somehow. Why don't you stick to your slaves?'

By way of reply the slave leader released his captive and nodded to Haemor. Before Brond could so much as scramble to his feet the giant had seized him by the ankles and tipped him upside down. With a bellowing laugh he shook the wretched thief for all he was worth. All manner of loot spilt out of his pockets on to the ground, including various tinker's tools and a fine ring.

'That's Oswain's,' cried Peter, who had come running across. He bent to retrieve the ring and slipped it in his pocket. Karador stripped off the stolen cloak, and Oswain's precious sword.

'What have you done with him?' he growled at the hapless bandit.

'I dunno,' he protested. 'Cryls came snoopin' afore we could finish the job. We got out fast.'

By now quite a crowd had gathered. Karador glanced around. They were drawing too much attention to themselves. He motioned to Haemor to let the thief go, which he did, sending a flying kick after him.

'Let's get out of here,' Karador ordered. 'There's too many people about.'

By early afternoon the party was safely back in the slave commune. Clea was beside herself with joy and relief at being reunited with her husband and daughter. In fact, everybody was thrilled with the news.

But Clea's delight instantly turned to sadness when her husband confided that he was determined to set out at once in order to find Oswain. She burst into tears and refused to be consoled. Karador didn't know what to do.

It was Danir who came to his rescue. 'Listen,' he said. 'Clea's right. You should be by her side. She's been through an awful lot these past few days.'

'But I gave my word I would help,' Karador protested. 'I can't let those children down.'

'Let me go instead,' Danir insisted. 'And I've got an idea.' He quickly explained his thinking.

Ten minutes later Danir and Hercules were

ready to go. The hound was taking a good sniff at Oswain's cloak.

'Here, take Oswain's ring,' said Peter. 'It'll help identify you if you find him. And it may have some power to help him.'

Hercules gave a yelp to say that he was ready.

'Good huntin', chum,' barked Tatters.

'Thanks, old boy,' Hercules replied. And with that, he and Danir were off.

They made their way to the inn where Peter and Sarah had stopped with Oswain. It took the hound very little time to pick up the scent and he was soon hot-footing it through the twisting, turning streets of the city. They had little difficulty finding the room where Oswain had been taken.

'Well done,' enthused Danir. 'Now where do we go?'

Hercules sniffed around for a few moments. And then he was off. The trail was easier to follow now and it was all Danir could do to keep up with him. It led to the temple steps.

'Oh, no, not again!' groaned Danir.

Being the day before the feast, many people were going in and out of the temple carrying various offerings. Danir decided to mingle among them. He quickly purchased a small bundle of sacred corn from a nearby tradesman and ascended the steps with an impatient Hercules.

'Slow down, boy,' he whispered. 'We've got to look inconspicuous.'

Hercules led him straight into the main triangular arena where the great gods stood. Danir was relieved that they hadn't got to break into Zarbid's study again. He looked around him. There seemed to be no place where a prisoner could be kept. For a moment he thought that perhaps the hound had lost the scent.

But Hercules knew what he was doing. He led Danir past the altar and towards a small alcove in the stone wall. Almost out of sight was an iron gate. The dog went up to it and then looked expectantly at Danir. With a cautionary glance, he slipped into the shadowy alcove. There was someone behind the gate.

'Are you Oswain?' he whispered.

He heard the rattling and scraping of chains and saw the figure drag himself to the bars.

'Yes,' he hissed. 'Who are you?'

'My name is Danir and I'm from Karador,' he replied. 'You won't know him but Peter and Sarah are with him. We're friends. I've brought this to prove it.' He passed Oswain the ring.

'Then Peter and Sarah are all right,' Oswain breathed. 'Elmesh be praised!'

'I daren't stop long, but we'll find a way to get you out,' promised Danir. 'Karador is good at doing that.'

Just then he heard a cry. A soldier was running towards him.

'I've been spotted,' he gasped. 'I must run for it!'

The soldier's cry soon alerted others. Within seconds armed guards were coming from all directions. Danir dived into the crowds, scattering them everywhere as he made for the exit. He ran as fast as his legs could carry him but he was outnumbered. Two of the guards had cut off his escape and stood barring the way with drawn swords. The others were only metres behind him. Danir hesitated.

Then to his delight Hercules came bounding

through the crowds and ran straight among the legs of the two soldiers in front of him. He caused such confusion that they both stumbled and fell. Danir seized his opportunity and shot past them. Within moments he had shaken off his pursuers and completely disappeared from sight.

It was late afternoon by the time he and Hercules reported back to Karador and the others. They were overjoyed at the news that Oswain was still alive, even though he was chained up in the temple gaol.

'Did well there, mate, didn't yer?' said Tatters to his companion.

Before Hercules could reply, a runner came with news that Surin's army was on the move. Vast numbers of soldiers had been seen leaving the city in full battle array.

'He's wasted no time,' observed Karador grimly.

'This is terrible,' cried Sarah. 'How can Elmar and the Great Forest survive without Oswain or the Ice Maiden? They'll all be killed! What are we going to do?' Tears welled in her eyes as she thought of Trotter's cottage falling beneath the onslaught of Surin's mighty army.

'I don't know,' said Peter. 'But we must do something.' He looked glumly in Karador's direction. 'We're completely stuck without Oswain,' he said.

The slave leader looked him straight in the eye. 'Then there is only one thing to do,' he said. 'We must get Oswain out tonight!'

Chapter Thirteen

A KNIFE IN THE DARK

Surin was feeling very pleased with events and ate his evening meal with relish. Zarbid sat opposite him in the private dining room. There were no other guests.

'The army looked magnificent, your Majesty,' said Zarbid.

'It is true,' replied Surin through a mouthful of food. 'Seldom have I seen the troops so well prepared or so eager for battle. Murg was right. I have kept the men idle too long.'

'But now the time has come,' Zarbid smiled. 'May you enjoy the fortune of the gods.'

'And the death of all our foes,' cried the king. He raised a goblet of wine. 'To victory!'

'To victory,' echoed Zarbid.

'You know,' said the king, wiping his mouth, 'all this is due in no small part to yourself, Zarbid. I have often been impressed with your powers but on this occasion you have excelled yourself. First Karador . . . .'

'But that was due to Balgus and the Cryls,' Zarbid protested.

Surin brushed the objection aside. 'Come Zarbid,

you know me better than that. Balgus would not have succeeded without your help. It is too modest of you to let him take the credit. Especially when you have captured not only the Ice Maiden but also Oswain himself.'

'It was the will of the gods,' Zarbid replied reverently. 'They have decreed that now is the time for Kraan's greatest victory.'

'And victory it shall be,' exclaimed Surin as he rose. 'But first I must visit the one who has thwarted that possibility for so long. Take me to Oswain!'

It was dark by the time Surin and Zarbid reached the temple precincts. Their footsteps echoed along the empty stone corridor which led to the triangular arena of the gods. The night was crisp and clear and the dread altar gleamed cold under the starlight. Shadows of deepest purple draped the tall stone walls and carved flagstones.

Zarbid indicated the alcove to the far side of the altar. 'We have him there, your Majesty,' he informed Surin.

'Hm, I thought you would have kept Karador in that cell,' said Surin. 'Isn't that your usual practice? Let the victim see the place of his execution for a day or two?'

'I, ah, have Karador elsewhere,' Zarbid lied. 'I did not want to risk a rescue attempt by his friends.'

Surin nodded curtly. 'So long as he is on that altar by daybreak when the crowds arrive,' he replied.

Zarbid stopped dead at this point and smote his brow.

'Your Majesty,' he gasped. 'I have forgotten something. In all the haste I have neglected to give Balgus instructions concerning Karador. Would you please forgive me and excuse my presence while I remedy the matter?'

Surin frowned. 'Very well, if you must do it at once,' he said. 'But give me the keys to the cell before you go.'

'The keys?'

'Well, you don't think I am going to stand by that stinking cell to speak to him, do you? I shall let him out into the fresh air. Besides,' he added, 'I want him to get a good view of our gods.'

Zarbid hesitated. 'Of course, your Majesty. How foolish of me,' he replied. 'Here are the keys. But do beware of Oswain. He is dangerous.'

Surin replied with a scornful laugh. 'On your way, Zarbid. A peasant king in chains is hardly a threat to Surin of Traun!'

Zarbid melted into the gloom.

'Oswain,' called Surin as he reached the cell. 'Are you awake Oswain, Son of the High King of the West, Ruler of the Great Forest? And prisoner of Surin, Lord of Kraan!'

There was a rattle of chains.

'Who is that?' called Oswain from the blackness of his cell.

'Oh, I forget. We have never met,' Surin mocked. He unlocked the gate and swung it back. 'Come outside, Oswain. It is I, Surin. Let us meet where we can see one another.'

Slowly and with the clanking of the heavy chains which they had fastened to his wrists and ankles, Oswain shuffled to the door.

'Greetings, fellow king,' Surin laughed when he saw him. 'You appear to be somewhat weighed down. Perhaps you should share with one who understands the burdens of kingship!'

Surin strolled away from the alcove towards a

solitary burning torch set in the wall leaving Oswain to stagger after him.

The king turned and peered at the strong features of his captive. He smiled grimly. 'I have long waited for this moment, Oswain,' he hissed. 'Always I have desired to conquer the South and for long years I had hoped my daughter would at last do my bidding. But it was not to be,' he spat, 'for you thwarted my plans, Oswain. But I have vowed vengeance, and now at last I shall have it!'

'It was not I who foiled your evil designs, but Elmesh,' Oswain replied evenly. 'And even now he will frustrate your plans.'

Surin laughed out loud. 'What folly you speak!' he cried. 'No land has ever withstood my might. True, I bide my time, but when I strike it is death to all who stand in my way! Your land will fare no better.'

Oswain smiled.

'You do not believe me?' jeered Surin. 'You think your god is able to deliver you? Come with me.'

He seized the torch from its bracket and escorted Oswain to the centre of the stone courtyard. The flickering flame fought feebly against the oppressive shadows thrown by the three huge monoliths which guarded each point of the triangle. Oswain's chains clanked with a hollow sound on the flagstones as they came to a halt.

His captor turned with a dramatic swirl of his cloak.

'You talk of your god, Elmesh,' he cried. 'He is nothing! These are real gods; gods of wealth and power and fertility.' He swept his arm around the arena. 'Igur, Damil and Oris, these I worship!' he cried.

Oswain followed their soaring forms; many-faced stone monsters they were, stretching their barbarous claws into the night sky.

'Forget your god,' Surin sneered. 'Soon your people will worship these.'

Oswain continued to gaze upward, but his eye had strayed far beyond the ghastly forms of Surin's gods. El-la, the star of Elmesh, gleamed like crystal against the velvet backdrop of the heavens. He smiled to himself. Then abruptly he looked Surin straight in the eye.

'I find your gods are rather too small,' he said quietly.

'Proud words, Oswain,' Surin scowled. 'But will they be so proud when I fling at your feet the corpses of your parents and that accursed daughter of mine? Will your words be so proud when you are bound to that altar and slowly sacrificed to the gods you so despise?'

Oswain remained silent.

Surin looked upon him with disdain. 'Back to your cell,' he ordered. 'You are hardly worth calling a foe!'

They had just reached the shadow of the alcove when it happened. There was the faintest rustle behind them. Oswain's keen ears picked it up at once. He spun round. A knife blade flashed as it plunged towards Surin's unprotected back. With a cry of warning, Oswain swung his manacled fist in its direction. He struck the attacker's arm just as the blow fell. Surin cried out and staggered to his knees clutching his shoulder.

But Oswain leapt upon the assailant and quickly pinned him to the ground. The knife which had stabbed Surin clattered away to one side.

Surin stared open-mouthed at the scene.

'So much for your gods,' Oswain said grimly. 'The knife was meant to kill you. Who is this man?'

Surin picked up the guttering torch and brought it close to his assailant's face.

'Balgus!' he exclaimed. 'What treachery is this?'

The chief of the Cryls stared in wide-eyed horror at the face of his king. He knew he had failed and only one fate awaited him. There would be no mercy.

Breathing heavily because of his wound, Surin seized Balgus by the throat and glared menacingly into his eyes. 'You shall surely die for this,' he snarled. 'But as to the manner of your death, I shall judge it by what you say now. Who is in this with you? How many other treacherous scum are there? What did you hope to gain?'

'Forgive me, Sire,' Balgus gasped. 'It was not my idea. Zarbid made me do it.'

'You lie,' spat the king.

'But it is true, your Majesty,' Balgus croaked. 'Zarbid intends to kill you and take the throne for himself. Why do you think you are alone here tonight, with your army removed from the city?'

'What proof do you have for this wild story?' Surin demanded.

'I would have had evidence enough, for I signed a document to pledge my part in Zarbid's plot. It was in return for him capturing Karador.'

'Then I will see this parchment,' snapped Surin.

'Alas, you cannot, Sire, for it has gone,' wailed the hapless Balgus. 'It was taken when Karador escaped. We expected it soon to be in your possession. That's why we attacked tonight.'

At this Surin's eyes narrowed. 'But Zarbid told

me he had to go and get ready for Karador's sacrifice tomorrow,' he breathed.

'It seems you have been fooled by your own trusted adviser,' Oswain observed dryly. 'What this man says is true. I already knew that Karador was free.'

Surin glanced sharply at Oswain then returned his gaze to Balgus. 'Where is Zarbid now?' he demanded.

'He will arrive here at any moment with his priests and all the Cryls,' Balgus gasped. 'We were to proclaim him king. Oswain was to be blamed for your death.'

Surin winced from the pain of his wound. His face was white. He looked up at Oswain and his eyes took on a hunted look as the realization of his position hit him.

'I am a doomed man,' he said grimly. 'What can I do? My army is gone, I do not even have a sword, and I am wounded.'

'There is always Balgus' dagger,' offered Oswain not very helpfully. 'Or you could try calling on your gods, of course.'

'Pah! And what good will that do?' Surin grimaced. Sweat glistened on his brow. He looked desperately into Oswain's face. 'You must help me,' he gulped.

Oswain held out his manacled hands and smiled. 'So Surin of Traun asks aid of a prisoner in chains,' he said. 'Then Surin had better release these chains, hadn't he?'

Surin looked doubtful.

'Come,' said Oswain. 'I have saved your life once this night. I might as well do it again!'

Surin took the key from his pocket and, with

some reluctance, handed it to Oswain. The ruler of the Great Forest released his bonds and stretched his limbs with relief. Surin, still crouched over Balgus, eyed him suspiciously. The fallen dagger was next to Oswain's feet. Suddenly, Surin darted for it.

Oswain leapt back instinctively and, in that same instant, Balgus seizing his chance rolled clear, and promptly fled from the temple.

'That was a rather foolish thing to do, wasn't it?' said Oswain. 'You forget, Surin, that my kind do not go back on their word. I said I would help you.'

Surin was silent. He didn't know what to say.

Oswain wasted no more time. 'Come on,' he urged, 'or we're both dead men. How bad is your wound?'

'I've had worse,' replied Surin with a glance to his shoulder. 'It's only a light flesh wound, thanks to you.'

'Then let's go!'

The two kings ran from the arena and along the corridor. They reached the steps just in time to see the light of hundreds of burning torches as Zarbid and his men marched on the temple. They were coming from all directions.

'Go for the weakest point,' whispered Oswain. 'Where there are the least number of lights. Look, over there!' He pointed to the left. 'Come on. Surprise is our only weapon.'

The two men crept down the steps with their backs to the wall. In moments, it would be light enough to see them.

'Now!' cried Oswain. And with that they charged full tilt into the small number of Cryls advancing on their left. The ploy worked and they broke through.

But immediately the chase was on. They hared in and out of the narrow city streets, often having to turn back because they could see torches coming towards them. The net was closing in swiftly, Oswain breathed up a prayer to Elmesh.

They fled down another alley. Surin pointed ahead to a small stone archway. 'Catacombs,' he gasped. 'In there. It's our only chance.'

One Cryl was almost upon them. Surin turned suddenly and kicked him hard. The man howled and fell. Surin tried to get his sword but Oswain grabbed the burning torch the man was carrying.

'This will be far more use,' he yelled. 'Now come on!'

Surin left the sword and followed Oswain through the tunnel entrance.

The catacombs were a honeycomb of underground passages and Oswain blindly led the way, taking a turn here and a turn there. Their footsteps sounded hollow as they ran and they could hear the sound of their pursuers hard on their heels.

How long they ran, he didn't know, but at length he stopped for a moment and listened. The only sound to be heard was that of their own heavy breathing and the thudding of his heart.

'I think we've lost them,' puffed Surin.

Oswain looked around him in the guttering light of the torch. It was then that he realized they were totally lost. And Surin had the dagger in his hand.

Chapter Fourteen

HAIL, LORD ZARBID!

Zarbid was almost beside himself with rage when he found out what had happened.

'You fool, Balgus. You utter incompetent fool!' he screamed. 'We have lost everything. First Karador and now not only Oswain but the king as well!'

Balgus cowered before Zarbid. They were standing in the temple court by the pile of discarded chains which had so recently bound Oswain. The chief of the Cryls had changed the story slightly, telling Zarbid that he had seriously wounded Surin and had engaged in a life and death struggle with Oswain, from which he had only just escaped. He did not tell the Sorcerer that he had confessed everything to Surin.

But Zarbid was no fool. He knew what had really happened. 'I ought to kill you for this, Balgus,' he grated. 'You have ruined everything and thwarted the plans of the gods. This is blasphemy!'

'But it's not all my fault,' Balgus protested lamely. 'You could have done it yourself.'

'Pah!' spat the Sorcerer. 'I wish I had. But I thought I was leaving it to an expert!'

Zarbid was angry, but his scheming mind was also thinking fast. He turned on Balgus. 'How many know that it was Surin who fled with Oswain,' he demanded.

'Only one got really close enough to see,' Balgus replied, relieved that the attention had moved off him for a moment. 'The rest just knew they were chasing two men. I have the Cryl who saw Surin waiting alone.'

Zarbid's eyes glinted. 'Good. I want him silenced,' he snapped. 'Kill him before he can talk.'

Balgus nodded dumbly.

'I also want the city gates closed and a watch kept on all the entrances to the catacombs. Anyone who comes out is to be killed without question. Is that understood? And I want only your most trusted men on the job. My priests will seal the temple until the feast starts tomorrow. You yourself will come to me at dawn for further instructions. Now get out of my sight.'

Balgus retreated to do Zarbid's bidding, relieved that he still had his life.

Zarbid paced the courtyard, deep in thought. After some time, he descended into his underground lair and approached the black altar upon which still lay the casket containing the unconscious Ice Maiden. Raising his hands in the air he began slowly to chant the names of his gods.

'Igur, Damil, Oris . . . Igur, Damil, Oris . . . Igur . . . .'

Gradually, a pale light began to glow above the altar. Zarbid sank to his knees. The air grew heavy with the smell of incense. Then the figure of Malik appeared, hovering in the ghostly light.

'Master, I am your servant,' whispered Zarbid

reverently. 'What must I do next?'

The old hermit gazed vacantly into space. Then he spoke. 'You have done well, Zarbid. Others have failed and they must be punished. But you are in the will of the gods. Tomorrow you will be king, do not fear.'

'But how will I explain Surin's death?' asked Zarbid. 'I have no corpse to show the people.'

'Is not the casket of Surin before your eyes?' replied the hermit. 'Why should it be otherwise to the people? The will of the gods is all that matters. Do not fail us Zarbid . . . .'

A deep thrumming filled the underground cavern. The figure of Malik vanished and slowly the pale light became blood red. Then a voice, terrible, like no other Zarbid had ever heard, spat these words.

'Kill and destroy! Show no mercy! Spare none!'

The sound and the light faded. Zarbid rose to his feet with a smile of evil satisfaction. He knew now what to do.

As the sun rose next morning, and before the crowds gathered for the feast, he gave Balgus precise instructions.

While all this was going on, Karador too had been busy. In the depths of the night he had emerged into the city through the secret entrance which Hercules had shown him. He went alone, armed only with a short sword and carrying a grappling hook attached to a length of rope. Besides that he carried some lock-picking implements.

Karador was an expert at releasing people from prison and always preferred to work in this way. Seeing that the main entrance was heavily guarded, he stole down a lane beside the temple. Minutes later he was scaling the outer wall with the aid of his grappling iron. He lowered himself into a narrow passageway which led him by many twists and turns to the centre of the temple. After checking that the coast was clear, he entered the court of the gods and slipped silently among the shadows cast by its towering walls until he reached the cell where he expected to find Oswain.

To his surprise, it was empty, and for a moment he thought with dismay that Oswain had been moved elsewhere. Then he spotted the pile of chains on the stones outside. A key still protruded from the lock on one of the manacles.

'It seems someone has beaten me to it,' he murmured with wonder. 'Or somehow Oswain has done it by himself.'

Karador hastened back to his friends. He noticed that the streets were swarming with Cryls and observed that they were especially guarding the known entrances to the catacombs.

'I guess that's where Oswain has fled,' he mused.

The others were delighted to learn that Oswain was no longer a prisoner.

'I still wish he was back here, though,' said Sarah. 'We can't really do much else without him, can we?'

Her two brothers agreed.

'We will have to search for him,' said Karador. 'He has no food and there is little water to be found. He could wander in the dark for ever down there.'

'Then we must start as soon as possible,' said Clea. 'Perhaps the dogs will be able to help us again.'

Tatters whoofed to say 'yes'.

'I want to help, too,' insisted Tarinda.

'And us,' chorused Peter, Sarah and Andrew.

Karador laughed. 'Very well. But we must stick

together. We'll make up one party. I'll get Danir and Haemor to organize the others,' he said. 'Now let's have some breakfast, and we'll be on our way.' Everyone brightened at the thought.

Shortly after daybreak, hundreds of people began to throng eagerly into the temple arena. This was the Feast of Oris, a wild, pagan affair during which the inhabitants of Traun committed all kinds of wickedness. And there was the added attraction this year of watching Karador being publicly sacrificed to the gods.

The great triangular arena was soon packed with expectant worshippers. Raucous, dismal-sounding horns announced the entrance of Zarbid followed by his priests. A hush fell over the audience.

Zarbid walked solemnly towards the high altar and mounted the steps. A murmur rippled through the crowd when they saw that the priests carried a large casket which they deposited on the altar.

Zarbid turned to face the people. His face was grim. 'People of Traun, worshippers of the great gods of Kraan,' he began. 'Today, on the Feast of Oris, I bring news of terrible tragedy.'

Another murmur ran through the crowd.

Zarbid's voice heaved with emotion. 'Surin our king is dead. Killed by the treacherous slave-leader Karador who escaped by dark magic and released our vile enemy Oswain. Together they struck down our gracious ruler in cold blood. Even now his mangled remains lie in this casket which you see before you.'

Stunned silence greeted this announcement. This was followed by a great howl of rage from the crowd. Many called for the blood of Karador and Oswain.

Zarbid held up his hand for silence. 'People of Traun, do not doubt that even now we search the catacombs whither these vermin have fled. We will not rest until they are caught. There will be no escape. We will have our vengeance. Vengeance, I say!'

The crowd took up the cry. 'Vengeance! Vengeance!' they chanted.

Zarbid motioned to Balgus who came and stood next to him. Then he raised his hand so that the people would listen.

'Hear me,' cried Balgus. 'I reached the king even as he was drawing his final breath. Alas, so foul was the attack that there was nothing I could do. But he gasped some dying words to me. I bring them to you now.'

Everyone waited while Balgus took a deep breath. 'Surin told me, "Zarbid is to be my successor. Tell the people to make Zarbid king."' He paused to let this sink in. 'People of Traun, what say you? Shall we ignore our king's dying wishes, or shall we elect Zarbid to this noble office?'

Councillors like Sneed looked uncomfortable at this, but the crowd needed no second bidding. 'Zarbid for king!' they cried. 'Zarbid for king!'

The Sorcerer raised his arm for silence. A hush fell over the whole assembly.

'Who am I, unworthy servant of the gods, a mere priest, to lead the great nation of Kraan? Who could follow after the illustrious Surin?' he protested. 'But I will bow to his greater wisdom and his dying wish. I will serve in his place.'

A mighty roar of approval arose from thousands of throats. Like the thunder of a great waterfall it drowned out all other sound. The priests began a chant. 'Hail, Lord Zarbid! Hail, Lord Zarbid!' they cried. It was taken up by the crowd.

'Hail, Lord Zarbid! Hail, Lord Zarbid!'

The Sorcerer leapt on to the altar where the casket lay and stretched his robed arms into the air with a look of ecstasy on his face. As he did so, a chill wind swirled and the whole arena was filled with a dreadful crimson cloud. People screamed with wild passion as the spirits of the gods took hold of them.

Throughout that day, the maddened crowds rampaged throughout the city filling its streets with debauchery and drunken violence.

Zarbid left the celebrations for a while and hastened to the palace. There he wrote a letter to Murg and stamped it with the king's seal. The message was simple.

'Noble Surin, our illustrious king, has been cruelly assassinated by Karador and Oswain. I have been appointed this day to reign in his stead. As my first royal act, I entrust you, Murg, to lead the armies of Kraan in exacting vengeance upon the foul kingdoms of the South, while I hunt the killers who still lurk in this city. Attack at once. Show no mercy, and do not rest until the blood flows in the streets of Elmar.'

The Sorcerer sent the letter by trusted horseman. He then posted notice that the funeral of Surin would take place the next day.

Murg was filled with a cold fury as he read the stark message. He at once called down all the dark powers of the gods to aid him in avenging his leader's death.

Within that same hour the mighty army of Kraan was on the move. And every soldier grimly vowed vengeance for Surin.

Chapter Fifteen

THE PALE LADY

Surin grimaced at Oswain, then laughed as he saw him eyeing the dagger. He thrust it under his belt.

'I see little point in trying to kill you down here,' he said. 'And in any case you saved my life. I do not understand it, but nor will I forget it. Strange it is that two mortal enemies should be thrown together in such a manner, do you not think?'

'The ways of Elmesh are often strange to mortal men,' Oswain acknowledged. 'But we will be immortal fairly soon if we don't find a way out of here. Do you know these tunnels?'

Surin shook his head. 'Alas, I have never ventured into the catacombs. I leave that to the Cryls when they are hunting runaway slaves or other criminals.'

'Then we are lost unless one of us can remember which way we came,' Oswain replied. He glanced at the flickering torch. They would soon be without light.

Surin swore. 'Curse Zarbid! And curse Balgus, too! What a fool I was not to uncover their schemings until it was too late,' he fumed. 'No doubt they now control the city while we are left to rot in these accursed tunnels!'

'I will pray to Elmesh,' Oswain said calmly. He gave Surin a quizzical glance. 'Will you pray to your gods?'

Surin looked at him as though he were mad. 'Gods have their uses,' he said. 'And the priests can draw on their power. But it is not for the likes of even a king to address them himself, nor yet to expect any help. No, we are on our own in this,' he concluded.

'Your gods are very different from mine,' Oswain replied. 'Why, even the simplest peasant-child can talk to Elmesh and know he is being listened to.'

'Such speech is foreign to my ears,' Surin confessed. 'I do not know of such gods.'

'Maybe you will come to know him,' said Oswain with a slight smile.

Surin gave a cynical laugh. 'I am a warrior-king. All I understand is the power of the sword, of conquest and victory. Your god sounds too good for my kind. And too soft!'

'We shall see,' Oswain answered. 'I shall pray in any case.'

Surin listened as Oswain called upon Elmesh to come to their aid. Nothing happened.

'Perhaps he doesn't have power down here,' he sneered.

'Elmesh has power everywhere,' Oswain replied shortly. 'Come on, we'll go this way.'

They walked for a long time along the endless rocky tunnels, helped only by the light of the torch. Occasionally they turned to the right or to the left, but they were never sure of their direction. For all they knew they might have been going round in circles.

'This is ridiculous,' Surin complained. 'We're getting nowhere.'

'I agree,' Oswain replied.

'So much for your god!'

They plodded on without further comment until they came to a tunnel bearing off to the left. They both felt a faint breeze on their faces.

'This could be a way out,' Oswain exclaimed. 'Let's follow it and see.'

They hastened along this tunnel and both felt a tinge of hope for the first time in hours. But then disaster struck. Oswain was leading the way and holding the torch when all of a sudden a gust of wind from a small crevice in the rock blew the flame out.

'Oh, no!' he gasped.

Surin swore loudly. 'Now what do we do?' he grumbled. 'We have no way of even seeing where we're going.'

'All we can do is keep following the direction of this breeze,' Oswain answered glumly. 'Let's hope it leads somewhere.'

And so they stumbled on in the inky blackness, trailing their hands against the walls of the tunnel in order to keep their bearings. It was a nerve-racking business and after a while they both began to feel the strain. To make matters worse, they each thought they could see lights dancing before their eyes.

'Confound the darkness!' cursed Surin. 'I don't think I can take much more of this.'

Just then Oswain stopped dead and reached out his hand to grasp his companion's arm. 'Look!' he whispered. 'Do you see that light? There's someone or something up ahead of us.'

'I have been seeing lights before my eyes for the past hour,' Surin answered scornfully. 'It's the way this darkness affects you. You are imagining things.'

'No, I'm not,' Oswain insisted. 'Look for yourself. What do you see?'

Surin blinked and stared hard. 'I see a pale figure,' he said slowly. 'It looks like a woman dressed in a long robe. But I can see right through her.' Then the realization hit him. 'It's a death-wraith!' he cried. 'By the gods, I don't like it, Oswain. We must not continue this way. I fear no flesh on earth. But this, this is different.'

'She's coming towards us,' Oswain observed.

'Then flee!' yelled Surin.

'No, wait. There is another way,' Oswain replied.

Standing square in the tunnel he called out to the advancing figure. 'I am Oswain, Son of the High King of the West, Ruler of the Great Forest and servant of Elmesh. With me is Surin, king of Traun. If you be sent to guide us, then we will follow, but if it be to deceive, then know that Elmesh will be your judge.' He took a deep breath and cried in a language which Surin had never heard. *'Yahrepsur ge sharendar. Torangula semareh poreti za!'*

The white figure halted, then slowly turned and beckoned them to follow.

'Don't go!' Surin cried hoarsely. 'She will lead us to our doom.'

'We are doomed here, anyway,' Oswain replied bluntly. 'But I feel she has been sent to guide us. I am not afraid. I will follow. You must do as you wish.'

'You can't leave me here alone,' Surin yelled.

'Then follow me and let us see where the pale lady will take us,' Oswain answered.

So, the two men followed the spectral figure. Oswain strode confidently, but Surin cowered all the way as deep-seated fears and superstitions rose to the surface of his mind. To his further discomfort, their path led steadily downwards, and through so many twists and turns that he knew they could never hope to retrace their steps. His sense of foreboding increased with every step they took. But still Oswain insisted they follow the pale gliding figure.

Then, all of a sudden, they rounded a large bend and found themselves at the top of a huge cavern. The rock glowed with a crimson light whose source lay far below. And before their feet fell a slender spiral staircase which wound deep into the bowels of the earth.

'It's the staircase of the dead. It leads to the abyss!' cried Surin. He stared wildly at Oswain with fear-crazed eyes. 'Curse your Elmesh! Curse this wraith! I will not venture further.'

Oswain glanced down at the woman. She was descending the dizzy stairs and beckoning them to follow. He hesitated for a moment, and then made up his mind.

'I do not fear the abyss, for Elmesh is with me,' he declared boldly. 'I will walk this path.'

It was at this point that Surin finally realized how useless his own gods were to him. They gave him no such confidence as Oswain had. Wearily, he agreed to follow.

'If I die, I die,' he said with resignation.

The staircase seemed to go down for ever and with each step Surin became ever more assured of his fate: he would never return from here alive. But Oswain had no such problems. He felt strangely alert and was quite fascinated by all that was happening to them. Somehow he sensed that this was in the purposes of Elmesh.

After a long giddy descent they came to a platform in the stairs. Though the spiral continued downwards into the unknown, a slender bridge led from this platform and into a hole in the cavern wall. To Surin's relief, the pale lady led them in that direction.

Upon crossing the bridge and entering the cave, they found themselves once more in the darkness of a tunnel. And not far ahead was the sound of running water. Their guide led them on. Quite suddenly, she disappeared from their view around a bend. The noise of the water was by now quite loud. Moments later, as they rounded the corner themselves, they saw the reason why.

They had arrived at a small cavern, on the far wall of which was hewn a round hole like some kind of rough window. Behind this roared a waterfall which glowed with a silvery-blue light. The pale lady stood beside the window and beckoned. Oswain at once made to go towards her but she motioned him aside with a wave of her hand. It was Surin she wanted.

He refused to budge.

'Is this some devilish trickery of yours, Oswain?' he growled. 'Why else would she want me but not you?'

'I assure you it is no plot of mine,' Oswain said. 'And I do not think she wishes to harm you. If she had so wanted she could have done that long ago. I think you should trust her.'

With great reluctance, Surin cautiously advanced. His eye was on the spectre all the time. She indicated that he should stand before the waterfall. And then, to his bewilderment, she simply drifted into the rock and vanished from his sight.

Chapter Sixteen

WHAT SURIN SAW

Surin stood gazing at the glittering cascade. The rushing of the water filled his ears. He was transfixed. Then he became aware of another sound. He could hear music. It was like nothing he had ever heard before; a high, unearthly, bell-like melody. And it made him shiver.

Then the waterfall began to draw aside like a curtain. Though he was so far underground, Surin found himself staring into the endless depths of space. It was as though he stood on the very brink of his own world, with nothing between him and the millions of brightly-glowing stars which spanned the vast expanse of the heavens. The sight made him feel giddy and he gripped the rock to steady himself.

His eye was drawn irresistibly to one star in particular. Oswain would have recognized it at once. El-la, the star of Elmesh, gleamed like a globule of molten silver. It outshone all the others and Surin was captured by its light.

Behind him Oswain stood motionless and watched. But Oswain never saw what Surin saw, nor heard the Voice which spoke into his heart. For then there flashed before the warrior-king the faces of all whom he had wronged in his quest for power —a thousand men and women whose lives had been ended by his sword, a multitude of children made orphans, slaves who bowed beneath his yoke, good men ruined by the favours he bestowed upon the bad. They came and came, the haunting, agonizing and accusing victims of his reign. And there passed before him, too, the sight of his own murdered wife and of his disowned daughter, Alena.

'These all had names, and lives, and loved ones,' the Voice accused. 'You never heeded that.'

'But it was necessary,' he argued back. 'War is war. To rule I had to destroy. There is no other way.'

Then other faces and other scenes passed before him. These were of innocence; of families gathered around the hearths in their homesteads, of children playing in the streets and free-born farmers carrying in their harvests, of palace courts where all were welcome and none was despised for his lack of wealth, or education or power. Nobody had fear in their eyes. Surin sensed that he was looking upon the lands of the South.

'But it is weakness thus to rule,' he protested.

'Is love so weak?' the Voice demanded, and Surin fancied he could see a man lay down his life for the friends he loved.

Now he felt weak and all his proud violence collapsed in that moment. For the star shone upon him still, and love was in its light. Deep sobs welled up within the broken man and tears streamed from his eyes. For in that light was a fire that burned the evil from his heart, and in that light was a warmth that thawed the iciness of his soul. Surin knew he would never be the same again.

The stars began to move and soon they were rushing downwards past his eyes with dazzling speed. Then he felt water. It splashed cold and fresh upon his face until he was drenched to the skin. The waterfall flowed once more.

Surin turned towards Oswain. His spray-soaked face was wreathed in smiles. Gone was the age-old hardness and pride. He felt young and clean instead. Then to a wondering Oswain he held out his arms in peace.

Realizing what had happened, Oswain hastened to embrace him. 'My brother!' he breathed. He had no doubt that Surin had met with Elmesh. For a long time they sat and talked of what it meant.

'I have much to learn, and much to change,' Surin concluded at length. 'I shall need your counsel for many years!'

Oswain laughed and rose to his feet.

'Then first we must return to the city,' he said.

Surin agreed. 'But how do we get back?' he asked. 'We have no guide.'

'If Elmesh brought us to this place, then he can surely lead us out,' Oswain replied. Then he frowned. 'The question is, how will he do it?'

Just at that moment, both men heard the clatter of a falling stone.

.   .   *   .   .

Karador led the way as his party set out on their search for Oswain. All four children accompanied him, along with both Hercules and Tatters. Haemor and Danir had set off in different directions with their own parties. At Clea's insistence they all carried adequate food and water between them, as well as a good supply of brands for spare torches. 'You don't know how long it might take for you to find him,' she said.

Karador also took several coils of stout rope, and chalk to mark their way. Even though they had the dogs with them, he was taking no chances.

Everyone set out with a sense of urgency. Surin's army was on the move and there was no time to lose.

But after several hours of walking the twisting, branching underground paths and calling Oswain's name every few hundred metres, they began to grow discouraged.

'This is hopeless,' said Andrew. 'We've walked for miles and not a sign of him.'

'How far could he have gone?' Sarah asked.

Karador shrugged his shoulders. One never knew in these tunnels. That was the problem.

'I suppose it's not worth dividing up?' Peter suggested.

'No, we stick together,' Karador insisted. 'We'll only divide if we have to.'

So far they had kept to paths which ran more or less on the same level, but eventually their route brought them to a small cliff at the foot of which the path dipped away very steeply. Karador hesitated.

'You don't think he could have fallen down there, Daddy, do you?' asked Tarinda.

'Possibly,' her father replied.

'Are there more paths lower down?' Andrew wanted to know.

'Yes, but I have never walked them. People who have talk of strange creatures in the lower reaches of the catacombs.'

'Do you believe them?' Peter asked.

'I don't know. But that's not going to stop us now,' he replied. 'We'll use the ropes and go down.'

Under Karador's direction, they made the ropes fast with iron pitons which they hammered into cracks in the rock. He felt it wise that they should not all make the descent and insisted that Andrew and Tarinda together with Tatters should remain at the top of the cliff in case there was any difficulty.

'It's all very well for you, old chap,' Hercules complained to Tatters as they lowered him unceremoniously in a rope harness.

'Never mind, chum. Just fink of the privilege of finding 'im while I'm stuck up 'ere,' Tatters rejoined cheerfully.

There was something different about the lower tunnels; as though they had entered a world of long ago. It made Hercules' coat bristle a bit, though he couldn't say why. They found evidence of ancient mine-workings and steps which always led them deeper into the bowels of the earth. Nobody knew who had carved them; it was a mystery whose answer lay deep in history.

They were halfway down one of these flights of stairs when Karador thought he heard voices. Just then, Sarah tripped and sent a loose stone clattering to the bottom.

'Shush,' hissed Peter, who had heard the voices himself.

They proceeded cautiously through the gloom to the base of the stairs. Then, just as they reached level ground, they walked slap-bang into Oswain and Surin who rounded a corner from the opposite direction.

'Oswain!' cried Sarah. She flung herself into his

arms, followed by Peter.

'My, I'm so glad to see you both!' he exclaimed.

'And are we glad to see you?' retorted Peter.

They were interrupted by the sudden hiss of a sword being drawn from its scabbard. Everyone whirled round to see Karador crouched with a burning torch in one hand and his sword at the ready in the other. His eyes blazed.

'What is this treachery?' he growled. His eyes darted accusingly from Peter to Sarah and then to Oswain.

'What's the matter, Karador?' Peter cried in alarm.

'Do you not know who this is?' he snarled.

The children shook their heads dumbly. He pointed his sword at the man who stood behind Oswain. 'That is Surin,' cried Karador, 'the one who imprisons and kills my people. I thought you were my friends. But you have deceived me. You serve Surin of Traun!'

Oswain stepped towards him and held out his hand in peace. 'What you say is not true, Karador. Nobody has betrayed you.'

'Then what are you doing in the company of Surin?' Karador demanded.

'It's a long story,' Oswain replied. 'But of this you may be sure. Surin is no longer your enemy.'

Karador kept his sword at the ready while Oswain explained what had happened to them in the deep catacombs. It seemed a fantastic story to the slave-leader and he was not convinced.

Just then, Surin stepped towards him and at the same time withdrew the dagger from his belt. Hearts beat faster and the children wondered for a moment whether Oswain had somehow been fooled. But the king turned the dagger and offered it by the handle to Karador. He took it wonderingly.

'This is certainly not the Surin I know,' he said.

'What Oswain says is true,' Surin said quietly. 'I have met Elmesh. I confess I do not yet understand it, but I believe I have this day become one of his servants.'

Karador hesitated and then slowly lowered his sword. 'There is no war or hatred between true servants of Elmesh,' he said cautiously.

'Long have I harried you and your people,' Surin confessed. 'Your bondage has been my doing, to serve my arrogance. Now I see that no man should be made the slave of another. I, Surin, beg your forgiveness, Karador.'

Tears came to Sarah's eyes as she heard these words.

'I have had cause enough to hate you,' Karador replied, looking Surin squarely in the eye. 'But your words ring true. For the moment, I will trust you.'

He stretched out his arm in peace and grasped Surin's hand. Hercules barked happily.

Oswain nodded sagely. 'Truly, Elmesh brings peace through strange means,' he marvelled.

'Well, here am I a slave-leader among kings,' Karador laughed. 'It is not fitting for me to lead this party further.'

'It is hardly likely that I am a king any longer,' said Surin ruefully.

'And I am your servant when it comes to finding the way among these caves,' laughed Oswain. 'No, I think you are still in charge, Karador!'

And so the party retraced their steps to the foot of the cliff.

'Won't Andrew and Tarinda be surprised?'

said Sarah.

'You bet,' Peter replied.

But when they reached the cliff, although they found the ropes still secured, there was no sign of the children or of Tatters. They called loudly, but there was no reply.

'I wonder what can have happened to them?' said Karador with a worried frown.

'We'd better get up there quick and find out,' Oswain answered grimly.

Chapter Seventeen

THE SECRET ENTRANCE

'This is boring,' Tarinda complained as she and Andrew sat waiting for the others to return. 'I'm getting fed up! Can't we do something?'

'Your dad told us not to move,' Andrew reminded her.

'I know. But at least can't we run up and down the tunnel, or something?' she insisted.

'I suppose you can if you want,' Andrew replied. 'I'm happy sitting here.' He lit another torch from the one which was guttering out.

Tarinda fished around in her pocket. She brought out a small ball of wool. 'How about playing throwing?' she offered brightly.

Andrew wasn't really interested, so she played with Tatters instead and soon had the dog scampering up and down the tunnel searching out the ball of wool with his nose. 'Better than sitting round doing nuffink,' he thought.

As is often the case with such games, they gradually began to move further and further away as Tarinda threw the ball a little bit harder each time. Soon they were almost out of sight.

'Hoi, don't go too far,' Andrew called. 'Come

back a bit.'

"S'all right,' called Tarinda.

She gave the ball one last throw as hard as she could and laughed as Tatters shot off to retrieve it. But he didn't come straight back. Instead, she could hear him snuffling about in the darkness.

'Come on, silly dog!' she yelled.

He replied by starting to bark. Andrew cocked his head. 'What is it, Tatters?' he called.

'I think he's found something,' Tarinda cried.

Andrew came running with a torch and together they hastened towards Tatters. They found him sniffing and pawing at the wall. Andrew peered closer. To his amazement he could see a faint glow of light through a chink in the rock.

'What is it?' whispered Tarinda.

'Some kind of room, I think,' Andrew replied. 'It's not daylight.'

It was then that they both noticed that a block of stone had been carved to fit loosely into a hole in the tunnel wall.

'Do you think we can move it?' Tarinda asked excitedly.

'Worth a try,' Andrew agreed.

Together they heaved and pushed, and to their delight it began to shift. Before very long, and after much puffing and panting, they had manœuvered it clear to reveal a small hole leading into a candle-lit room. Tatters growled sullenly.

'I'm going to take a look,' Andrew declared boldly, and promptly disappeared into the room.

'Do be careful,' Tarinda cautioned.

Seconds later, his face peeked through the hole. 'It's Zarbid's lair,' he gasped. 'We've found a secret way in!'

Tarinda joined him at once, followed by a more reluctant Tatters. He remembered what had happened the last time he had been here.

'Look, the Ice Maiden's still there,' Tarinda exclaimed.

'We've got to tell the others as quick as possible,' Andrew declared.

'We'd better get back to the cliff then,' said Tarinda. 'Do you think we should go down after them?'

Before Andrew could reply, they heard voices calling their names.

'I think they're back,' he cried. 'Come on!'

They had just crawled through the secret hole and into the tunnel when Karador and his companions came upon them.

'Where have you been?' he demanded. 'I told you to wait by the ropes. You'll be knowing about this, my girl!'

'B . . .b . . .but, Daddy! We've found something,' she protested.

Before Karador could say anything else, Oswain came forward. 'Andrew!' he cried warmly. 'How tremendous to see you!'

'Hello, fancy meeting you here!' the boy replied, as though it was an everyday occurrence.

'Cheeky as ever, I see,' Oswain laughed. He looked at Tarinda. 'What is it you have found?' he asked gently.

She gave him a pert smile. 'You must be Oswain,' she said. 'I'm Tarinda. Come and look at this.'

Feeling very important, she led Oswain and her father through the secret hole. Karador recognized the place at once.

'There is the Ice Maiden whom you seek,' he said

to Oswain, and pointed to the casket.

Oswain's eyes lit up. 'This is wonderful,' he exclaimed. 'Well done, both of you!'

'You must thank Tatters for that,' said Andrew, feeling rather proud of his dog.

'That was a good piece of nose work, old bean,' said Hercules to his friend.

'Praise indeed, that is. Comin' from you!' Tatters replied. He felt very pleased with himself even though he couldn't see what was going on.

'We must release her, if we can,' said Oswain.

'Not here,' cautioned Karador. 'There may not be much time. Let us take the casket to safety and then open it.'

Reluctantly Oswain agreed, and so he, Karador and Surin carefully lifted the coffin from Zarbid's hideous altar and eased it through the hole in the wall. It just made it. Once through to the other side, the men shouldered their burden and, after pushing the rock back into place, started towards the slaves' hideout.

Thanks to the chalk marks and the dogs' noses they had no problem retracing their steps. Even so, it was still quite a long journey and the coffin was heavy. By the time they arrived back to the slave commune they were quite exhausted. The sky above was darkening and they entered by lamp light.

Their arrival caused quite a stir and everybody stopped what they were doing in order to watch this strange procession. It was not so much the arrival of the coffin which caused such a buzz, as the entrance of Oswain and Surin. That the hated king should be in their hideout was incredible and many watched with trepidation, fearing that somehow Surin must have Karador at his mercy. Everyone fell silent as Karador climbed on to a sturdy table in order to address them.

'You may wonder indeed at the strange sight before you,' he began. 'I wonder myself. For the impossible appears to have happened.' He paused. 'Surin is at peace with us.'

Gasps of incredulity greeted this statement, and not a few looked quite unbelieving. Had Karador lost his mind, or fallen under some evil spell?

Surin stepped forward. He looked nervous. 'It is true,' he said. 'We are at peace. That is not my doing but the work of Elmesh. Yes,' he continued in answer to their astonished looks, 'the true One has revealed himself to me and shown me my follies. I have renounced my former gods and my former ways.'

At this news a few cheers and a smattering of applause arose from within the assembled company. They had suffered much at Surin's hands and were not easily to be convinced by his words, however fine they were.

Surin continued in a solemn voice. 'Many here I have wronged. I do not know how to repay the debt, especially to those who have lost loved ones. You are entitled to whatever revenge you wish, for I am at your mercy. All I do is humbly ask for your forgiveness.'

Some wept at these words and did find it in their hearts to forgive him. In doing so, they received comfort from Elmesh and from that day on there began the healing of their many griefs and sorrows.

Karador addressed Surin. 'We are not willingly people of violence. Whom Elmesh forgives, we seek to forgive also, hard as it will be for some of our people. On their behalf I stretch out the hand of peace to you.'

Surin bowed his head low as he took the proffered hand. Then he stepped back among the others.

Karador continued. 'Much there is to say concerning the events of this day, but I must hasten to introduce one who is to be highly honoured among us as truly a noble servant of Elmesh. He is Oswain, the Son of the High King of the West, and Ruler of the Great Forest.'

Loud applause greeted Oswain as he stepped forwards. Karador ushered him up onto the table to stand beside him.

'My friends,' Oswain began. 'I bring greetings from the South, from Elmar, city of my father, and from the Great Forest where I dwell. It is a great honour for me to be among you. I knew nothing of your existence but came with my friends seeking the Ice Maiden who for so long has protected my kingdom from the forces of Kraan. Here I expected to find only enemies. Instead, I have discovered friends.' He smiled. 'More I will not say at this moment of the strange purposes of Elmesh which have caused our paths to cross and, beyond my wildest dreams, have reconciled me to my archenemy. For I have a more urgent task.'

He indicated the casket.

'Within this lies the one whom I have sought. I do not know if she still lives, for a terrible magic struck her down. If she is dead, then I fear for all our lives. But if she can be revived then there is hope for each of us.'

He glanced at Karador. The leader motioned the people to gather in a large circle around the casket.

'The hour has come for you to open the casket, Oswain,' Karador said solemnly. 'May Elmesh be with you as you do so.'

Oswain walked across to where the casket lay and placed his hand upon the handle of the lid. Then, slowly, he began to lift it.

Chapter Eighteen

ALENA RIDES TO WAR

An awed hush fell over the slave commune as Oswain raised the lid of the coffin. No one moved. Nobody spoke.

Sarah had her hands over her eyes and peeped fearfully through her fingers, ready if needs be to shut out the sight at once, for she dreaded what might remain of the Ice Maiden if she were dead. Even Oswain hesitated before allowing himself to look.

But look he did, and there, encased in ice, lay the black-swathed figure of the one whom he had sought so earnestly these past days. He motioned those near him to gather round. Even as they did so, the ice began to melt with an unnatural speed and the coffin rapidly started to fill with water.

'This is Zarbid's magic,' growled Surin. 'Quickly, Oswain, get her out if you would have her to live!'

Oswain tried at once to lift the Ice Maiden from her frozen tomb but he found to his dismay that he could not do so. In minutes, her head would be under the water. He motioned urgently for his friends to help tilt the coffin, but some awful power had fused it to the floor; even their combined

149

efforts could not budge it. Frantically, his fingers tore at the black bindings which covered her face but the material proved too strong. This was Zarbid's dark doing and even Karador's proffered dagger failed to make any impression upon it.

'What are we going to do?' Sarah cried in alarm. 'She'll drown!'

'Your sword!' Peter exclaimed. 'Where's your sword, Oswain?'

Karador snapped an order and, moments later, Danir came running with the weapon. Oswain seized the scabbard and unsheathed the blade. It blazed with a bright blue fire that made everyone shield their eyes; this was the blade which Elmesh himself had forged. Oswain at once applied it to the bindings. To his relief—and everyone else's—it cut easily through the swathes.

'Well done, Pete,' said Andrew.

They watched as Oswain gently uncovered the Ice Maiden's face. No one breathed a word as they gazed upon her pale, perfectly formed features. Sarah thought Oswain must surely fall in love with her at once.

She could have been carved from alabaster, so still she lay, and almost as white. Only a slight tinge of blue about her lips betrayed any colour. It was this that suddenly caused consternation, for even as they looked her skin was becoming bluer.

'She's not breathing,' gasped Andrew. 'Do something quick!'

But Oswain could only stare helplessly.

'Kiss her,' urged Sarah. 'That's what they do in all the fairy stories.'

Oswain gave her a puzzled look, but then bent and gently kissed the Ice Maiden's cold lips. They watched anxiously for signs of life. Nothing happened. She continued to grow even more blue.

It was then that Peter had another flash of inspiration. 'The ring!' he cried. 'Use the ring.' He remembered how once the crystal it contained had saved him from certain death.

Oswain touched the ring to her lips. And as he did so, strange words came from his mouth. *'Selementi camil sarestra, lameka poresi tamamora. Dorantel karesa!'* he called.

At once the Ice Maiden began to breathe. Slowly the blueness vanished and her cheeks began to colour, first pale, and then a delicate flush of pink.

'She lives! The Ice Maiden lives!' Oswain cried.

A great cheer arose from all around.

Oswain peered anxiously at her face. Her eyelids fluttered for a moment—and then they opened. To his immense joy, her face broke into a radiant smile.

'You are Oswain,' she whispered. 'I knew you would come.'

He nodded. For a moment, he had no words to say.

Then he asked her, 'What is your name?'

Sarah remembered that once the Ice Maiden had told them she could only reveal her name to the one she was to love.

The Ice Maiden looked deep into Oswain's eyes for a long time. Then gently she said, 'My name is Loriana.'

'Loriana,' he repeated. 'The Shining One.'

At once, to his amazement, the black bandages which encased her body began to dissolve away in the water. In moments, they were no more than drifting cobwebs of gauze. Oswain took her by the hand and gently assisted her from the watery casket. He saw then that on her third finger she wore a ring set with a crystal identical to his own.

She arose, resplendent for all to see in her snow-white gown, and as she did so an oyster-pink light began to radiate from her slender form. It seemed to pour from deep within her being and it bathed those around her with such a wondrous love that all fear fled at once from their hearts.

There they stood, the noble Oswain in his rugged strength and the fair Ice Maiden in her radiant beauty. Quite spontaneously, the assembly erupted into loud applause, and cries of, 'Hail Oswain! Hail Loriana!' filled the cavern.

'Truly, your journey was worth while,' said Karador, gazing in wonder at the Ice Maiden's beauty.

'Dismiss the crowd, my darling, before you get too entranced,' laughed his wife, Clea. She addressed Oswain and Loriana. 'It would be my privilege to provide food and drink for you if you so wish,' she offered.

'It would be our delight,' Oswain replied. 'I for one am starving!'

'I, too, am hungry,' said the Ice Maiden softly. 'But first I must greet three old friends who have played a part in my destiny.' She glided across to where Peter, Sarah and Andrew stood in a somewhat awestruck huddle.

But it did not take her long to put them at ease and soon they were chattering nineteen to the dozen about all that had happened to them. She nodded wisely as they told their tale.

'There is much to be done and soon,' she said solemnly. 'But there is something I would do at once.' She addressed Andrew. 'Bring your dog to me.'

Andrew's eyes lit up. He looked round for Tatters.

'Here, boy. Here,' he called.

Tatters' ears pricked up and he lolloped across to his master's side. The Ice Maiden stooped and gently took his head between her hands. He gazed sightlessly back at her and whined quietly.

'I understand,' she said. 'But do not fear the darkness any longer, nor the pain of silence. Elmesh is your light and your music.' And then she breathed upon his face.

The dog blinked and shook his head.

'Hey, I can see again!' he barked. 'And I can speak! Now ain't that marvellous?' He jumped into the air and for no accountable reason started chasing his own tail. Hercules barked encouragement.

When he had calmed down a little he padded across to the Ice Maiden and looked up seriously into her face. 'Fanks fer doin' that,' he said. 'I'll never forget it. Anyfink yer wants me ter do, well, just say the word and I'll be there.'

Tears of gratitude ran down Andrew's face, while Peter and Sarah were just fascinated to hear Tatters speaking.

'Oh, and just one more fing,' he said to the Ice Maiden. 'Can you make me mate 'ere speak as well?'

She smiled at him. 'Why, of course,' she said, and called him over.

To the delight of everyone present the same wonder worked on Hercules, too.

'I say, old chap, this is absolutely spiffing! I don't know how to thank you,' he said to Tatters afterwards.

'Don't mention it,' his friend replied airily. 'You gets what you asks for, that's what I always say!'

This happy event over, the company was soon seated at table and enjoying a well-earned meal. However, conversation quickly turned to events outside. This became urgent when a messenger arrived to report that Surin's army had been seen vanishing into the mountains. He told the strange tale, too, that each of the soldiers seemed enshrouded in a red halo, so that the whole army appeared as a sullen crimson fire.

'Then Zarbid is surely king in my place,' Surin said despondently. 'And I am too late to stop him.'

'What will happen, do you think?' Peter asked.

'Why, by dawn tomorrow they will be sweeping down the mountains and on towards Elmar,' the king replied grimly.

'That's awful,' exclaimed Sarah. She looked desperately to Oswain. 'What are we going to do?'

'My men are yours, Oswain,' interjected Karador. 'But we could never catch up with them now, even if we had the fastest horses in the kingdom.'

Oswain thanked him for the offer and then glanced at the Ice Maiden. They seemed to know each other's thoughts. 'We will seek Elmesh,' he said. 'There will be an answer.'

Thus he and Loriana excused themselves from the table. An hour later, they had climbed almost to the rim of the crater. Below lay the dim lights of Traun. Above stretched the star-spangled heavens. They gazed southwards towards the mountains. An ominous red star lay low on the horizon.

'Alas, the Naida will be powerless to stop them without my presence,' said the Ice Maiden.

Oswain directed her eye to El-la. 'But Elmesh is never without power. We must call upon him to intervene.'

Loriana smiled. 'You speak my thoughts, Oswain. Let us await his bidding. I know not how else to stop this war.'

   .   .   *   .   .

The innkeeper, Rolan, arrived dusty and dishevelled at the city of Elmar. The moment he stated his business at the palace gates he was ushered into the presence of the King.

He had ridden all night at the insistence of his wife, Suen. When three full days had passed and Oswain and the children had not returned from the mountains, she had urged her husband to follow Oswain's instructions to report to the palace.

He had taken Oswain's fine steed and ridden as fast as he could, leaving Suen and the children to follow by horse and cart. A sense of evil in the air made them reluctant to remain alone at the inn.

The Feast of Oris was just dawning in the north as Rolan swept through the gates of Elmar, and by the time Zarbid was being proclaimed King in the North, the council was in full session.

The King spoke gravely, 'I fear that war is almost upon us. Already I have enquired in the Tower of Visions. Your news is no surprise, good innkeeper. But we thank you for it, disturbing as it is.'

Rolan bowed. 'I am here to serve you in any way you see fit, Sire.'

The King acknowledged the offer graciously. He turned to the Lord Chancellor. 'How many troops do we have?'

'Few enough, Sire,' he replied. 'And ill prepared for battle. We have been at peace for a long time, and bloodshed is foreign to our ways.'

The King nodded sagely. 'Aye, that I know well. And I wish it were unnecessary to fight. But defend our people we must,' he said firmly. 'Though only Elmesh knows how we can even hope of doing so,' he added.

Then a new voice spoke. 'I will lead what troops we have. It is for me to face at last my natural father.'

All eyes turned on the speaker. It was Princess Alena. The young, golden-haired girl had jumped to her feet opposite her father.

'But child, surely it is fitting that I should lead the army?' the aged King protested.

'It is not fitting that one who is wise with years should play the fool by acting as a youth,' she replied, with rather more defiance than she had intended.

The King was taken aback.

'I. . .I'm sorry, Father,' she gasped. 'I had not meant to be rude. It's just that I don't want you to die in battle.'

'Nor I you, child,' the King replied softly.

'But Alena is right,' said the Queen. 'Terrible as it is, she must lead our army.' Her grey eyes filled with tears. 'I do not want you to do this, Alena, but what you say is true; the King and I are too old to go to war.'

'Then it is agreed,' said the princess with a glint in her eye. 'We march as soon as possible.'

At noon that day, Princess Alena donned her sword and mounted a white charger.

'Elmesh go with you, my child,' sobbed the Queen. 'I can scarcely hope that I shall ever see you again. But I pray it may be so.'

The King reached up and gripped her hand. 'All our hopes go with you, my dear. Though they be few enough.'

He glanced around at the few hundred horsemen they had gathered. This tiny army was no match for Surin's thousands. The old King smiled wanly. 'Do what you can, and do not be ashamed for what you cannot do. If we are all to die, let it be known that we did so with honour.'

'Thank you, Father,' she replied. 'I will entrust our ways to Elmesh. And who knows what he might yet do?' she added brightly.

And so the little army paraded out of the city, waved on by the anxious inhabitants who lined the streets. Resolutely, they headed north.

By late afternoon, they were in sight of the mountains. Rolan had met his wife and urged her to continue south. He would stay and fight. Tearfully, she agreed.

They camped at the edge of a broad field as the sun sank in the west. Tomorrow this would become a battleground which would decide the fate of thousands.

As darkness fell and the first stars began to appear, Princess Alena stood by herself looking northwards. She was preparing to face her father in battle the next morning, and for the first time she felt afraid. 'Please, Elmesh, I wish it were not so,' she whispered.

Her eyes strained towards the dark outline of the mountains. A dull crimson light burned on a high ridge. And low on the horizon a terrible red star began to rise. Alena shivered. The hordes of Kraan were already within sight!

Chapter Nineteen

MURG ATTACKS

It was still dark when the alarm sounded. Princess Alena awoke at once and rushed from her tent to see what the commotion was all about. She found an agitated guard pointing wildly northwards. Her eye followed his quivering finger through the darkness.

There like a lurid crimson gash slowly advancing across the plain she saw the full might of Surin's terrible army. She felt sick in her stomach and weak at the knees.

'What magic makes them like that, your Highness?' asked the awestruck guard.

Alena eyed the shimmering line grimly and then pointed to the sullen red star in the sky above. 'I don't fully know, but greater powers are at work than ever Surin could conjure up. I think vast destinies will be decided today,' she said. 'Rouse the troops. They will be on us by dawn.'

While the guard rushed to do her bidding, the princess continued to observe the approaching enemy. It was like a low bank of glowing red mist rolling towards them and she knew her tiny army would be completely overwhelmed unless they received help from outside. She scanned the skies in vain for sight of El-la, but strangely the star of Elmesh seemed hidden from view. She shivered. What if Elmesh did not save them? Supposing the red star was the stronger after all?

But Princess Alena was not one to give up easily. She clutched at her birth-stone, the famed Star-Pearl which hung about her neck. It gave her strength. 'It doesn't matter,' she said to herself. 'I can do only what I can do. The outcome is in Elmesh's hands. I will trust him, even if I have to die doing so!'

· · * · ·

Murg felt more confident than ever before as he approached the battlefield. Had he not led the mighty army of Kraan across the dreaded mountains single-handed? And no Naida to be seen! Zarbid had done his work well. Perhaps he would make a good king, after all. At any rate, Murg was determined to prove his worth to the Sorcerer. He would bring the South to its knees and utterly crush its leaders for ever!

Indeed, he couldn't wait to take his revenge upon Oswain's house for the treacherous murder of his own king, Surin. Hatred smouldered inside him like a volcano about to erupt, and he knew every one of his troops felt the same.

For this reason, he welcomed the strange power which had fallen upon them from the red star. Normally, such a thing would have terrified him, but not this night. He stared again, hard-faced, at the source of the unearthly sheen which hung over the army.

'Give us full vengeance, and we will do anything you wish,' he growled. The star responded with a stream of pure hate which poured into his very being even as he spoke. 'Prepare for the attack,' he cried to his lieutenants. 'We strike at sunrise!'

The word spread through the vast ranks stretched out across the plain. Swords hissed from their scabbards. Horses snorted as the smell of battle inflamed their nostrils. Harnesses jingled while spears and lances were set in place.

After this, a tense silence fell as the soldiers awaited the fateful order to charge. It was almost dawn.

·   ·   *   ·   ·

Princess Alena sat astride her charger. Behind her were mounted the soldiers that comprised her tiny army.

'Elmesh have mercy upon us,' she muttered. It was a prayer echoed in the hearts of every one of her loyal troops. The odds were overwhelming.

They seemed to wait for an age, watching all the time the shimmering red line. The air hung unusually heavy and it was difficult to breathe. Alena could feel her heart thumping.

Then it came. Just as the night sky was tinged blue by the onset of dawn. A single cry, followed by a mighty roar from thousands of battle-inflamed throats. The crimson cloud began to advance and a dull rumble of hooves filled the air.

'Here they come!' cried the princess.

She drew her sword and held it aloft. The blade

shimmered blue in the half-light and the sight of it gave courage to the brave company. They had little other comfort.

'Hold your ground until I give the command,' she ordered.

The princess was waiting until the enemy drew near enough for her to make a charge. She hoped that then they might at least break through the ranks once.

But to her dismay, she saw that rather than coming at her in a straight line, the outer flanks of the advancing force were sweeping round so as to enclose her little army. Within minutes, before she could think which way to turn, a vast ring of troops had been thrown around them so that they were completely encircled. Then Murg gave the final order and, with battle-cries rending the air, the cavalry thundered in for the kill from all sides at once.

Princess Alena knew they were defeated even before they engaged the enemy. There was no way they could hope to take on such a vast army. And now they could not even retreat. Despair filled her heart as she prepared for the worst. She wondered if Surin himself would smite her down—the final cruel stroke of the father who had disowned her.

But just then she recalled the parting words of her adoptive father in Elmar: 'Do what you can, and do not be ashamed for what you cannot do.'

The princess set her jaw firmly, 'I am not going to sit here waiting to be cut to pieces,' she declared. 'If I am to die, then it will be with honour.' And with that, she raised her blazing sword high in the air for what she expected would be the last time.

As she did so, to her utter amazement, a streak of

blue lightning flashed from its tip. She looked at the advancing enemy, expecting to see it smite one of the leaders. But it didn't. Instead, it shot away northwards far into the sky above the mountains.

Then, in the pale light of early dawn, she spied dark flecks rising above the peaks. She strained her eyes hard to make out what they were, while still the fire blazed from her sword.

A voice spoke at her side. It was that of Rolan, the trusty innkeeper. 'They're eagles, your Highness,' he exclaimed. 'White eagles. Lots of 'em. And they're coming this way!'

'I don't believe it,' said the princess in a dazed voice. 'It can't be, surely?'

The next moment a shrill, blood-freezing screech rent the air, and she was left in no doubt at all. 'It's Arca!' she cried. 'Elmesh be praised, we're saved!'

At that very second the first rays of the sun broke over the horizon and in their light a host of white eagles could be seen winging towards the battlefield. The sky was filled with their awesome screams, which echoed and re-echoed across the plain as they swooped downwards.

And behind them streamed a myriad trail of glittering, dancing stars. The air tingled with uncanny power and Alena shivered as she felt the hairs rise on the back of her neck.

Then she spied something else. There were people riding the two leading birds. And on the greatest of them was one whom she knew must be Oswain, for he had his sword drawn and it was between this and her own that the blue lightning blazed. Her troops recognized this, too, and a mighty cheer arose at the sight.

'Oswain! Oswain, my brother!' cried the princess.

'And never more welcome!'

Murg's army froze in mid-charge, still a hundred metres from their prey. Anguished faces stared upwards at the awesome spectacle. Then, to their horror, a stream of sparkling stars spiralled down to form a circle between them and Alena's army. Horses reared at the sight and many a rider was toppled. Others turned tail at once to desperate, fear-filled cries of, 'Aagh!! Naida!!'

But there was to be no escape, for more stars poured from the skies and ringed Murg's army about so that they were soon totally surrounded. Meanwhile, the eagles wheeled wildly over their heads, screeching for all they were worth. Panic ensued and in moments the invincible army of Kraan was in complete disarray.

The great eagle bearing Oswain fluttered gracefully to the ground in front of Alena. She leapt from her steed and ran towards her brother as he slipped from the bird's neck.

'Oh, I'm so glad to see you!' she gasped, half laughing and half crying, as she flung her arms around him.

'And I you, my sister,' he replied with deep feeling.

She turned to the mighty white eagle. 'Arca, you've come again in the nick of time. And with so many more this time.'

'It is the bidding of Elmesh, Princess,' he cawed.

'Then praise be to Elmesh!' she exclaimed.

She looked around at the tumult created by the other eagles and the Naida. 'B. . .b. . .but how?' she asked incredulously.

Oswain answered by pointing to an eagle which was coming in to land. Alena watched open-mouthed as the slender form of the Ice Maiden gracefully dismounted and came towards them.

'Let me introduce to you Loriana, the Ice Maiden,' he said proudly.

The princess looked from one to the other. 'Loriana. It's a lovely name,' she whispered. 'So my brother Oswain has found his true love at last. I'm so happy.'

The Ice Maiden smiled demurely. 'And I have found my love, too,' she replied. 'No longer am I bound to the mountains where last we met, Alena.'

'Nor I to the curse which then held me,' answered the princess. She laughed and flung wide her arms. 'I am well and truly healed since then!'

The two women embraced happily while Oswain looked on with a broad grin on his face.

'Joyful and timely as this meeting is,' he said at last, 'we must do something about all this.' He indicated Murg's panic-stricken army, still hemmed in by the Naida and harried by the eagles who wheeled overhead.

The Ice Maiden took his arm. 'Would you have bloodshed or peace?' she asked with a twinkle in her eye.

He looked at her askance. 'Why, peace, of course,' he replied stoutly. 'I have no pleasure in death, even of my sworn enemies.'

'Then raise your sword aloft, my dear,' she smiled. 'And such a peace will fall as you have never seen!'

He did as she bade. Then Loriana, the Ice Maiden, began a song of such mesmerizing beauty that Oswain and Alena felt they were drifting from the earth into a warm blue lagoon of perfect stillness. How long it lasted they couldn't say, but when it ceased and they looked about them in the cool light of morning, there was not a sound to be heard nor a movement to be seen.

Princess Alena's own troops all sat like statues upon their horses, both man and beast in a trance-like sleep. And in a broad ring a hundred metres distant, silent and still lay the whole army of Kraan, each man and horse stretched out on the ground.

'Are they dead?' gasped Alena.

'No, they sleep,' laughed the Ice Maiden. 'Look closely and you will see why.'

Even from this distance, the princess observed the reason; a twinkling star, barely visible in the morning light, hung over every soldier and horse.

'The Naida,' explained Oswain simply.

'Your own troops will be refreshed when they awake,' the Ice Maiden assured her.

'And these?' queried Alena, indicating the Kraan army. 'What of these, and what of Surin?'

'Ah, um, Surin is a long story,' Oswain began. 'Suffice it for the moment to say that you will not find him here. We'll explain it all as soon as we can.'

'And as for his army, well, it is time they learned the ways of peace,' said Loriana. 'And for that we will give them the instruments of peace. Come.'

They walked together to where the nearest troops lay. The Ice Maiden uttered a command. Then to the startled eyes of Oswain and Alena, the Naida began to dance in the sunlight. Soon the air was filled with their tinkling music as round and round they spun in a dizzy, glittering halo above the sleeping soldiers and horses. And as they did so, the strangest thing began to happen. All the weapons were refashioned before their very eyes.

Swords became farming tools—spades, forks,

166

ploughs, hoes and scythes—and spears turned into craftsmen's tools so that soon the ground was littered with hammers and chisels, planes and saws. Lances and shields became artists' equipment and scientific apparatus, while helmets turned into musical instruments. Soon there was not a weapon of war to be seen.

'That's incredible!' marvelled Princess Alena.

'And will they have the skill to use these?' asked Oswain.

'That they must learn for themselves,' replied the Ice Maiden. 'And, alas, they may unlearn it too.'

'What do you mean?' asked the princess.

'The instruments of peace will quickly again become the weapons of war if the people listen not to the voice of Elmesh but to the gods of Kraan,' she replied solemnly.

Oswain nodded, 'Then it is to Traun we must go, if we would destroy the real cause of all this trouble,' he said.

And so it was that within the hour, the two bemused armies were on their way to their respective homes. Not a drop of blood had been shed between them. Alena's troops marvelled at their deliverance and gave thanks to Elmesh. Murg and his men rode silently, escorted by the Naida and clutching their changed weapons with dazed looks on their faces.

Meanwhile, high over the mountains soared a hundred white eagles, and on the leading three rode Oswain, Loriana and Alena. In Arca's fierce eye a light glinted as he flew. He had grim business to do in Traun before the day was over.

Chapter Twenty

THE JUDGEMENT BEGINS

Surin tossed and turned on his bed in the slave commune. He had scarcely slept a wink all night. So many things were running through his mind. Would Oswain and the Ice Maiden be in time to stop his army from slaughtering Princess Alena and her forces? How does a king behave when he becomes a follower of Elmesh? And what could be done to regain Traun from Zarbid's evil clutches?

This last question disturbed him so much that at length he arose from his bed and staggered bleary-eyed into the main cavern. It was almost dawn.

'It's no good,' he said to himself. 'I cannot simply remain idle. I must do something about Zarbid.'

He made his way to Karador's quarters. Clea was already pottering about. She greeted him with a broad grin.

'My, you look a sight for sore eyes,' she said.

He smiled ruefully. 'Now you see Surin of Traun as he really is,' he replied.

'I have always seen Surin of Traun as he really is,' she replied knowingly. 'I take it you want Karador? I'll call him.'

Ten minutes later the two men were discussing

the matter together over breakfast.

'I have loyal people in Traun, I know it,' said Surin. 'They have been tricked into thinking I'm dead, that's all. I must get to them.'

'But how will you deal with Zarbid?' Karador queried through a mouthful of bread.

'I don't know . . . . Wait a minute. Didn't you say you had some parchment or other signed by Balgus?'

Karador nodded.

'Then we have the means to unmask their treachery. Once Sneed and others see that I'm alive and read the parchment they'll give us all the support we need,' Surin replied with a light in his eye. 'We'll rally enough men and march on the temple.'

'You're sure?' Karador asked, a little doubtful.

'Of course I'm sure,' the king answered emphatically.

Karador was on his feet. 'Then let's do it,' he said. 'I'll round up a couple of dozen men and we'll enter the city through the secret tunnel. Nobody will be expecting us to come that way.'

The first thing that struck them as they emerged from the basement cellar was the foul-smelling reddish mist which hung in a pall over the city. It was so thick that the morning sun had entirely failed to penetrate it, and houses appeared as no more than brown shadows looming over the narrow dank streets. The air was cold and clammy.

Under Surin's guidance the small company crept stealthily towards Sneed's house. Their spirits felt the despair of the city. Every so often they came across a body lying in the gutter. Drunks staggered by, singing sad songs. Many windows were smashed and doors hung crazily from burgled homes. Somewhere a woman screamed.

'The fruit of the gods,' murmured Karador.

'I see it now,' Surin answered grimly.

Before long, they reached Sneed's opulent mansion. The City Treasurer disliked being disturbed so early in the day but when he saw who it was his piggy eyes nearly popped out of his podgy head.

'Surin!' he gasped. 'But I thought you were dead!'

'One of Zarbid's lies, I'm afraid,' Surin answered shortly.

He began to explain what had happened over the past few days. He also showed Sneed the evidence of Balgus' treachery and told of Zarbid's part in it.

Sneed flopped into an easy chair. 'Why, this is incredible. I hardly know what to say,' he wheezed. He eyed Karador and the men with him. 'I . . . I will, of course, give you all the assistance I can, your Highness. Please be assured of that,' he said.

Surin looked at him curiously. 'I'm sure you will, Sneed. I'm sure you will,' he murmured.

'Well, just what are we going to do?' Karador demanded. 'We're going to need as many men as possible if we're to take on Zarbid and Balgus. Where are we going to find them?'

Before anyone could reply, the door swung open with a loud crash. Everyone spun round at the sound. But even as they did so, the room was flooded with Cryls armed to the teeth with swords, spears and crossbows. Karador and his men went for their swords.

'I wouldn't do that if I were you,' said a stern voice from the doorway. 'You're completely outnumbered, so drop your weapons.'

Karador fixed Surin with a penetrating stare. Were his worst suspicions to be realized? Had the king tricked them after all? His eye turned upon the speaker. It was Balgus.

The Cryl chief glanced from Surin to Karador and back again. 'So we meet once more,' he sneered. 'How foolish to think that you could come back here. Did you think to obtain help from Sneed?' He laughed. 'That fat old bag was half in it himself. Wanted a share of the loot, he did.'

Sneed lay back gulping like a stranded goldfish under Surin's penetrating stare. 'I . . . I didn't know he was going to assassinate you, Sire,' he stammered.

'No matter,' Surin replied. Then he added, to his own and everyone else's amazement, 'I forgive you anyway, Sneed.' He turned to Karador and motioned towards the Cryls. 'No more bloodshed, my friend. Put up your weapons. We'll leave our fate to Elmesh.' Then he added. 'There was no trickery. I am as much a prisoner as you are.'

'How right you are!' interjected the mocking voice of Balgus.

Karador shrugged his shoulders with a wry grin. 'Truly, Surin is a changed man,' he marvelled, and he threw his sword to the floor.

'Take them all away,' Balgus snapped. 'And this time there will be no escape. To the temple! Our king, Zarbid, is waiting!'

.   .   .   *   .   .

'I don't like it,' said Tatters. 'Reckon they're gonna get themselves in a right load of trouble, if they ain't careful.'

'I could not agree more, old boy,' his friend Hercules replied.

'Then 'ow about us following them, like. Just ter keep an eye on fings?'

'A capital idea,' Hercules agreed. And with that, the two dogs padded out of the slave commune and into the tunnel which led to the city.

They managed to follow the scent, in spite of the foulness of the atmosphere, and soon they were within sight of Sneed's house. In fact, they arrived just in time to see the commotion as Surin, Karador and Sneed, together with their men, were being bundled into the street by Balgus and his Cryls.

'Hey, I don't like the look of that, old boy, do you?' growled Hercules.

'Too right I don't, mate,' replied Tatters. 'Told yer they'd get into bovver, didn't I?'

'Better follow them. But keep your distance,' Hercules advised. 'Those crossbows are deadly, even in this fog.'

'What are we gonna do?' Tatters asked. 'We can hardly take that lot on by ourselves can we?'

'No, but I've an idea,' Hercules replied. 'Listen, old chap, you keep on their trail. I'll be back soon. They're probably taking them to the temple, but bark three times every hundred paces so that I'll know where you are, just in case.'

And with that the hound was off, leaving Tatters to trail the Cryls and their prisoners.

Hercules' guess was right and it wasn't long before the company was marching down the street that led to the temple precincts. Tatters gave another three barks.

Almost immediately he was answered by

Hercules. The next instant, the air was filled with the raucous sound of baying hounds as dozens upon dozens of shadowy shapes shot past Tatters and poured into the square. They made straight for the Cryls.

The mongrel was not to be outdone. 'Wayhey!' he shouted, and with that threw himself into the fray for all he was worth.

The Cryls didn't know what hit them. Sheer weight of numbers and their surprise emergence from the fog caught the soldiers completely off guard. And these hounds were not playing. They went in hard with jaws snapping and claws bared. It was all the Cryls could do to defend themselves.

Karador needed no second bidding. 'It's Hercules and Tatters,' he cried. 'Come on! Let's make a break for it!'

'Stop them!' screamed Balgus, as he saw what was happening. He seized a crossbow and aimed it at Surin's fleeing form.

'Oh, no you don't, mate,' growled Tatters.

He leapt at Balgus and sank his teeth into his arm. The Cryl chief howled and dropped the bow. By the time he looked up, nursing his wounded arm, his prisoners were nowhere to be seen. He cursed loudly.

As soon as he saw that the prisoners had escaped, Hercules called off his hounds. 'Okay, chaps,' he bayed. 'Mission accomplished. Return to base.'

Within moments, the pack had melted into the mist, leaving the dishevelled and wounded Cryls to sort themselves out as best they could, while Balgus stormed up the temple steps to demand an edict from Zarbid ordering the death of every dog in Traun.

. . . * . . .

'Tatters and Hercules have gone, too,' Andrew puffed as he ran up to Tarinda.

'I bet they're looking for my dad and the others,' she replied.

'Huh, you'd think they would've told us first,' Andrew grumbled. 'I'd like to have gone as well.'

Just then Peter and Sarah came wandering over.

'Hello, you two,' said Sarah. 'Hey, you don't half look glum, Andrew. What's up?'

'Oh, nothing,' he replied. 'It's just that everyone's doing something except us. I mean, there's Oswain and Loriana conquering armies on eagles, and Karador beating up Zarbid, while we're just stuck here waiting. And now even the dogs have got in on the action.'

'I know what you mean,' Peter agreed glumly.

'Well, why don't we do something?' Tarinda insisted. 'I mean, what's to stop us sneaking into the city ourselves?'

'It's probably too dangerous . . .' began Sarah. But she shut up as soon as she saw the others' looks. 'Oh, all right,' she agreed. 'Come on, then.'

So the four children sneaked off down the same tunnel as the others. The trouble was, they didn't know the way so well and somewhere along the line they took a wrong turning. Soon they were quite lost.

'This is ridiculous!' Peter exclaimed after yet another useless detour. 'We could wander down here for ever!'

Tarinda was more cheerful. 'Don't worry,' she said brightly. 'I've often got lost in here. You always find your way out sooner or later.'

'So long as your torch doesn't go out,' Andrew muttered.

'Oh, no, I've done it in the dark as well,' she laughed.

Just then they heard a deep rumble far beneath them. The ground trembled under their feet and the sound echoed and boomed all around them.

'What on earth was that?' exclaimed Peter. 'It sounded like a bomb going off.'

They all stood stock still. Then, in the silence, they heard a faint hissing sound. It grew louder and louder.

'Look!' cried Andrew. 'There's some kind of mist coming towards us.'

The others peered through the gloom. Sure enough, a white cloud was billowing down the tunnel towards them. In spite of the anxious cries of her companions to be careful, Tarinda ran forward to have a look.

'It's not mist,' she shouted. 'It's steam. And there's water as well, and . . . and it's boiling!'

'Then let's get out of here quick!' Peter yelled. 'It must be some kind of underground geyser. Run for it!'

The four children raced back the way they had come as fast as their legs could carry them. The hissing sound was growing very loud indeed and the earth trembled again under the impact of another underground explosion. Steam began to billow from all different directions.

'Oh, dear, we're going to be boiled alive!' wailed Sarah.

'Not if we can help it,' Peter panted. 'Come on, let's keep aiming upwards. It's our only chance.'

On they plunged through the steam, scarcely able to see where they were going in the flickering light of their torches. They came to a junction of several paths.

'Which one do we take, Pete?' gasped Andrew.

His brother looked around him helplessly. 'I'm not sure,' he began. At that moment, he was interrupted by the bark of a dog.

'It's Tatters!' Andrew shouted exaltantly. 'This way!'

A minute later, they ran into the dog and indeed the whole company which had escaped from Balgus' clutches. Quickly, Peter explained what had happened.

Karador looked grim. 'We'd better get back as fast as possible,' he said. 'I fear the judgement of Traun has begun.'

With no further ado they ran for their lives. Within minutes they were pouring into the main cavern. Every man ran straight to his own family's quarters.

Karador shouted at the top of his voice: 'Everybody get out. Leave your possessions and make for high ground. Quickly now or we're dead!' He ran in search of his wife.

Mums and dads—many carrying babies—children, old people and teenagers fled for the tunnel which led from the cavern and up to ground level. They poured like ants from a crevice and at once began to scramble up the side of the volcano. By the time Karador and Clea left—and they were the last—boiling water was already bubbling into what had been for so long the home of their people.

Clea grasped her husband's jerkin and looked up at him with big, anxious, tear-filled eyes. 'Karador, what are we going to do?' she whispered. 'We've lost everything!'

Chapter Twenty-One

A NEW DAY DAWNS

'Thank goodness you discovered what was happening,' puffed Karador as he clambered up to join the children. 'It would have been dreadful if we'd all been caught in that boiling water.'

Clea was right behind him. 'Elmesh has been merciful,' she panted. 'Though you shouldn't have gone without telling me. Anything might have happened.'

Tarinda looked suitably crestfallen. 'Sorry, Mummy,' she said. Peter, Sarah and Andrew mumbled their apologies too.

Clea laughed at their solemn faces. 'Don't worry. I'm not really cross,' she assured them. 'Especially now that we're all safe.'

Surin came clambering across the rocks to join them. They were about three-quarters of the way up the side of the volcano and most of the others had climbed nearly as high. Even though they had certainly lost their homes and possessions, everyone was out of danger.

'It's quite a view, isn't it?' Peter observed as he looked around him. He pointed south to the mountain range which divided the two kingdoms, 'Remember climbing over that lot, Sarah?'

'I just hope Oswain and Loriana got to the other side in time,' Sarah answered.

'So do I,' interjected Surin. He knew only too well how powerful his army was. They would surely have massacred Princess Alena and her troops by now unless Oswain had stopped them.

'I'm sure it's all right,' Andrew chipped in. 'Arca's never failed yet. Hey, wasn't it fantastic seeing him with all those others? I always thought he was the only one.'

'He's still the greatest, though,' Sarah remarked stoutly. 'I just wish we could have gone with them as well.'

They were interrupted by Tatters, 'Hoi, you lot, look down there,' he barked.

They gazed down upon the city of Traun. It was completely enveloped in reddish cloud and not a building could be seen. But streaming from the gate they could see hundreds of people fleeing for their lives and making for the side of the volcano.

'The water must be coming up through the catacombs,' said Karador.

'Then we're not the only ones to have lost our homes,' Clea remarked.

'It's the cleansing of Traun,' her husband replied solemnly.

Just then, the sky was filled with an ear-splitting screech. Everyone whirled round. The noise came from the south.

'Look!' cried Peter. 'It's the eagles!'

Everyone on that mountainside watched in awe as the flock of giant birds winged towards them. Karador noticed too that heavy storm clouds were rolling in rapidly from the west.

Three birds wheeled off from the rest and swooped towards them. They carried Oswain, Loriana and Alena. Moments later, they fluttered down to land on the very rim of the volcano. Their passengers slipped off their mounts as though there was some great hurry, and the eagles at once flew off to rejoin their companions in the sky.

Oswain was grinning from ear to ear as he leapt enthusiastically from boulder to boulder down to his waiting friends. 'Success!' he cried as soon as he was within earshot.

'Hooray!' shouted Sarah. She rushed across to hug him and was immediately joined by the others who filled the air with the babble of a thousand and one questions.

'One at a time,' he laughed as he sat down on a rock.

Surin did not join the huddle around Oswain. Instead, his eyes were upon Princess Alena who, together with the Ice Maiden, was progressing more slowly down the hill. It was the first time he had seen his daughter since she was a tiny baby. Then she had been known as Astar. He felt a lump rise in his throat and his eyes smarted as the fine young woman approached him. Loriana led her across to where he stood, but then withdrew discreetly to join the others listening to Oswain.

For a long time the king and his daughter said nothing. Surin stared at the golden-haired girl with the determined face. She gazed back at this powerfully-built man whom she both feared and respected. It was she who broke the silence.

'I have never known you,' she said, 'so it's difficult for me to call you Father.'

'I claim no right to that title,' he replied meekly,

'for I sought only to use you for my own ends; and when I could not, I disowned you and hated you.'

Princess Alena looked down at her fingers. Her eyes felt watery. 'My brother, Oswain, tells me that you have changed. Is it so?' she asked.

'I have met the One whom I was taught to hate,' he confessed. 'Elmesh has changed me and I have become his servant.'

'Then . . . then I greet you . . . in his name,' she choked.

'Oh, Alena, forgive me,' he cried. 'Forgive me the cruelty I have done to you.'

The dam of emotion burst and, with tears streaming down their faces, they fell into each other's arms. And there, as father and daughter embraced on that mountainside, with the storm clouds gathering and the people fleeing the doomed city below, their wounds began to be healed and their tears washed away the pain of many years.

While this was going on, something was happening over Traun. Thousands of people had fled and were swarming up the hillside like insects, desperately seeking safety, for the city, still hidden by the noxious cloud, was now surrounded by a vast lake of seething, steaming water. But what caught everyone's attention were the eagles. Led by Arca, they were wheeling in a great spiral above the red mist.

Suddenly, as though he had been awaiting a signal, Arca let out a terrible screech and plunged headlong into the very core of the cloud. The others streaked down after him and vanished into the mist.

Nobody knows what terrible judgement the eagles wrought upon Zarbid and Balgus in that awful temple. But when later the people returned to Traun they found no trace of either, nor any of their followers. And the three great idols, Igur, Damil and Oris, lay fallen and shattered beyond repair across a broken altar. The temple which for so long had ruled and corrupted the people of Traun lay in ruins.

But those who watched from the hillside knew nothing of this at the time. They simply had to wait anxiously while the red mist swirled over the city.

And then it started to rain. It began with just a few heavy drops, but soon the storm broke in full force. Water fell in torrents, blotting out everything from view. Lightning slashed through the skies and thunder rumbled angrily over the mountains. High on the hillside, the citizens of Traun huddled together as best they could and prayed for protection.

After about fifteen minutes the storm began to pass and, as the rain ceased and the thunderclouds rolled eastwards, they saw that the rain had entirely washed away the foul mist, so that they could now see the glistening grey roofs of the city. Then the sun broke through, and as it did so a hundred white eagles spread their wings and rose like a cloud on the wind. Their grim task was done.

Arca glided across to where Oswain and his friends stood soaked and awestruck. But he did not land. Instead, he let out one last mighty screech of triumph before winging off to rejoin the others. And the wistful crowds watched them chase the stormclouds, until they vanished from sight.

Several hours later, Oswain and his company were gathered in Surin's palace. The waters had receded as quickly as they had come, leaving the city cleansed of its filth. Zarbid and Balgus were no more. Sneed had promised not to be greedy again. And Murg was leading home a very different army from the one which had left the city to conquer the South.

It was something of a celebration at the palace, what with Oswain having found his Loriana and Princess Alena reconciled to her natural father. Food and drink flowed freely and there was a happy buzz of conversation.

Oswain took Surin aside and spoke with him. 'Karador and his people have no homes,' he said. 'Something must be done for them.'

Surin nodded and clapped his hands for attention.

'My friends, I have something important to announce. For many years Traun has used and abused the slaves whom Karador leads. We have built our wealth on their labour and sufferings. But it shall be so no more.' He addressed the leader of the slaves who stood with his arm around his wife's shoulder. 'I, Surin of Traun, declare you and all your people free, Karador. And may Elmesh bless your freedom.'

Karador smiled and Clea kissed him, her eyes brimming with tears of joy.

'On behalf of my people I gladly accept the freedom you give,' he replied with quiet dignity. 'And may your reign ever be blessed with peace.'

Everyone began to cheer. Surin held up his hand. 'That is not all,' he continued. 'Your people have no dwellings, and we owe you a great debt. I decree, therefore, that the temple ruins shall be razed to the ground and the land given to your people for ever.'

He was interrupted by Sneed. 'This is a noble gesture indeed, Sire,' he said. 'But who shall pay for dismantling the temple?'

Surin turned his eye towards the City Treasurer. 'You will, Sneed,' he said quietly. 'And you will pay the cost of building houses and workplaces for these people from whom you have made so much profit in the past.'

The fat treasurer blanched but under Surin's stern gaze agreed to provide all that was necessary.

Then, to the delight of all, Oswain and Surin signed a treaty of peace between their two kingdoms.

'A new day has dawned for the kingdom of Kraan!' exclaimed Surin. 'No more will we build by fear and bloodshed, but by love and co-operation. You'll have to teach us how, Oswain. And you, too, Alena.'

'We'll do our best,' Oswain smiled.

As for Peter, Sarah and Andrew, they knew it was time for them to return to their own realm. Everybody came with them to the Star-shaft where Andrew and Tatters had first met Tarinda.

'Goodbye, Oswain,' said Sarah. 'I'm so glad you've found your true love.' She blinked back a tear as she kissed him. Oswain smiled, and the Ice Maiden touched Sarah and filled her heart with a hope and joy which eased the pain of parting.

Peter and Andrew shook hands with everyone, and both kissed Alena and the Ice Maiden. Tatters and Hercules rubbed noses.

'Well, cheers, old pal,' said Tatters. 'Been quite an adventure, ain't it?'

'Rattling good, I would say, old bean,' Hercules replied. 'Take good care of yourself now, won't you?'

'I will, don't worry,' he replied. 'Oh, and I 'ope a

lot more of your gang gets their 'uman voice back like you,' he added.

Tarinda looked at Andrew from beneath her long lashes. 'I'm going to miss you,' she said shyly.

'Me too,' he replied awkwardly. Then, to Tatters' delight, he kissed her clumsily on the cheek before joining the others in the shaft.

The Ice Maiden and Oswain stood before the three children and Tatters. 'Farewell, my friends,' he said.

'Elmesh go with you,' added Loriana.

The next moment they felt themselves floating upwards as though in a dream.

'Oh! Ouch! That's my leg!' groaned Andrew.

'Well, get it off my neck then.'

'I will if you let go of my arm.'

The three children and Tatters were lying in a tangled heap on Andrew's bed. Tatters started to bark.

The next moment the bedroom door burst open and in strode their mother.

'Children! What on earth do you think you're doing?' she cried. 'Andrew's supposed to be ill!'

The tangled children looked up at her helplessly.

'Oh, Mummy,' Sarah sighed. 'If only you could understand!'

.   .   *   .   .

And far, far away in the enchanted glade in the Great Forest an aged badger gazed into the Star Pool.

'Well, well, well,' he wheezed. 'So everything

turned out just fine, after all!' He smiled to himself.
'Oswain will be back soon. I had better put the kettle
on!'

Hagbane's Doom

A tale of heroism, adventure, and the age-old conflict between good and evil

by John Houghton

Introducing...

Peter, Sarah and Andrew—three ordinary children caught up in an adventure that proves to be far from ordinary.

Trotter, Aldred, Stiggle and company—a band of lovable animals united in the fight against a wicked tyrant.

Hagbane—an evil witch who rules the Great Forest with a bitter hatred and an iron will.

Oswain—a prince whose destiny not even he will fully understand until he looks into the enchanted pool.

Children of all ages (and there's no upper limit!) will enjoy this gripping fantasy which portrays the power of love and goodness in the face of evil.

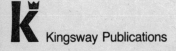

Kingsway Publications

Gublak's Greed

by John Houghton

Powerful forces are on the move . . .

Princess Alena runs away from home. She has the Star-Pearl with her –

Gublak the goblin wants it more than anything else in the world.

Oswain has a strange dream.

Peter, Sarah and Andrew again find themselves drawn into another realm –

Can they rescue the princess from Gublak's evil clutches?

What is her real identity? Why is the Star-Pearl so important?

Find the answers in this enthralling sequel to HAGBANE'S DOOM.

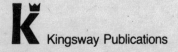

Kingsway Publications